Dedicated to

My Mother and Sister

Chapter 1
Celebrations and Holidays

Yesterday had been a fantastic, warm sunny Sunday just coming up to the end of May. On that morning, I had been jogging over the "*Sun Shadow Hills*". They were a really well-known beauty spot in the area and a particular favourite for many people who were into jogging. The reason I had taken up jogging was because I had retired from work a couple of years ago at the ripe old age of 62. I started just after I had retired after being told by a very good friend, who had been a trainer of athletes professionally for about 30 years, that if I started jogging now it would probably add an extra 10 years to my life. I have to say when you went jogging and you reached the summit of "*Sun Hills*" as we used to call them, you could pause and look down to see the River Sweet meandering through the countryside. The sight of it on a lovely sunny day was absolutely stunning. The immaculate thought that came into your mind was if there are sights to been seen like this then everything in the world must be perfect. Of course, that particular thought was absolutely stupid. So, brushing that thought aside we'll move on and enjoy as much as possible, of what life has to offer us. I continued my jogging and after returning to the foot of the "*Sun hills*" I had just over half a mile to go to our little cottage in the village of "Tipsy". I suppose really it would be a good idea if I introduced myself. My name is Stuart Grifford, I haven't lived a star studied life but I have enjoyed my life immensely. I have been married to my wonderful wife Nathalie for 38 years and we have raised two lovely girls, Anita who's 38 years old and, Paula whose birthday it was yesterday and she was 32 years old. Nathalie and myself have lived in our cottage for 17 years. I know it's a bit corny but there is a sign over the front door saying,

"*Country Cottage*" and yes, my wife and I did put the sign there and even after all these years we still smile at each other when we look at it and just think about what a total lack of imagination we had when we chose it. But of course, we both love the cottage dearly, and at least we didn't call it "*Primrose Cottage*". It took me about 12 minutes to jog the last stretch home, and when I arrived Nathalie was just pouring me a cup of tea. She could almost time me to the minute when I went for my jog, from the time I left to the time I returned. It was such a lovely day that we sat in the garden to have out tea, if the day wasn't so good we would sit in the conservatory. After drinking our tea and each of us telling how our morning had gone, it was time for us to get nice and clean, and then dress up ready to go out to celebrate Paula's birthday. There's four people in Paula's family including herself. There's her husband Daniel, a son named Jamie who's 12 years old and a daughter named Petra who is 10 years old. Of course, Anita will be coming with her husband Taylor and their twin boys aged 13 years old named Aden and Wesley. We were all meeting up on the Sunday evening in the reception area of the "*Goshawk Castle*" hotel at 7.30pm. We had a table booked for all ten of us at 7.45pm. At 7.40pm we were all present and ready to take our seat for our meal. Without boring you with the details of every moment that we each had during the meal, I will try to shorten the explanation by saying that the "*Goshawk*" had a very good reputation for high quality food and a very varied menu. I can therefore tell you that we all had a wonderful meal and a thoroughly enjoyable evening. Also, as far as family events go I don't think it could have gone any better. Nathalie and myself returned home to our cottage that evening about 10.15pm. We don't usually go to bed quite that early but as we had been out all evening we decided to go to bed straight away and have a little read and a chat before settling down. After having a read we then discussed a topic that we had been contemplating for quite a while. That was, what are we planning on doing for our next holiday. The problem we seemed to have whenever we talked about going on holiday in the past few years was, that because we had been married for 38 years we were finding it quite difficult to come up with somewhere new that we hadn't been to, and both of us wanted to visit. On this occasion, there seemed to be one favored destination. The only reason I can think of for us not having been before during our 38 years of marriage was because this particular place was probably about as far from England as you could travel or one of the furthest. Well at the end of the discussion we happily agreed that we would take a flight from Manchester airport to San Diego spend two nights there and then take a cruise ship to Hawaii. We would stay in Hawaii for two weeks and then cruise back to San Diego and there catch a flight back to Manchester. Nathalie was going to a local ladies' coffee morning first thing, so we agreed that whilst she attended the coffee morning I would go into the little town near our village and start making the arrangements to book our holiday with our favorite travel agents *"Happy Travel"* who we had been using for some years and we had actually become quite friendly with the couple who owned it. When we settled down and switched the lights off, I think we were both already quite excited. We both woke up fairly early to what seemed to be a rather pleasant Monday morning as far as the weather goes. Because we had woken up so much earlier than we actually needed to we began to have a little canoodle, but as all the little canoodles do it turned into a rather long canoodle than we had intended. Eventually when we did get up out of bed we both had to start getting ourselves ready to go out in quite a brisk manner. As I had said a bit earlier Nathalie was going to her coffee morning and I was going to the travel agents to start the ball rolling for our cruise. We both went out of the front door at

10.45am. When we reached the gate, we gave each other a little "I love you forever kiss" on the lips. My wife then walked up the lane and I went in the opposite direction down the lane towards our closest town which was called "*Potterford*". There were only about 5,000 residents who actually lived in "*Potterford*" and it is recorded in the town hall that the town originated about 500 years ago because there used to be a clay pit nearby and most of the local people living in the area used to make pots and vases to sell in the local market. Hence the area was called "*Potterford*". Now I do realize that this probably doesn't surprise quite a few people. I arrived in the high street about 11.10am. As you stood at the top of the high street you could look down the slight hill into a dip and then the road would climb up again the other side until it reached about the same height as where you were standing this side. On either side of the road there were only small shops, most of them being family owned shops. There were no large stores or big super markets, you had to go to the nearby city of Talken for larger types of shop. Right in the dip at the bottom of the high street there were three shops with scaffolding all along the front of them. There was on going work being carried out to repair the roofs of these three particular shops. The reason for this work was because we had gone through quite a bad patch of weather in March and some very strong winds had taken a number of tiles off the roof. The middle shop of the three was the travel agent that I was just about to visit. I walked down the high street on the left-hand side, in a fairly, brisk fashion. I suppose I was getting a bit excited about the holiday again. Directly outside the travel agents there was a pedestrian crossing with traffic lights, obviously they were there to help people to cross the road. Just when I was a few steps away from the travel agents and of course the pedestrian crossing I noticed there was a little old man, a pensioner, with a Zimmer frame crossing the road. He had got about three quarters of the way across. Just then the lights changed so that the traffic could start moving again. I could tell that the pensioner had noticed the lights had changed colour and he was visibly trying to get across the road faster, he was without doubt struggling to go any faster but presumably he was feeling embarrassed because he was holding the traffic up.

My immediate thought was, I'm only a few paces away I will have to go and help him. Instinctively I quickened my last few paces to reach him more quickly. Just as I reached out to help him everything went completely blank.

Chapter 2
A Choice of Destiny

Wow, I had no idea what had happened. As I opened my eyes I found myself lying on a single bed with just a single white sheet spread over me. I slowly looked around the room that I had I found myself in. It wasn't a particularly big room and although it was really bright I couldn't actually see where there was any light source coming from, either electrical or natural. There was what appeared to be a window frame on the wall to my right-hand side, but the inside of the frame was just a plain light grey colour the same as the walls all around the room. On the same wall as the frame was a rectangular shape that appeared to be a door but it had no frame and there was no handle. The rectangle was the same light grey colour as the rest of the room.

On the left side of the bed there was a small chair a light grey colour once again and it blended perfectly with the rest of the room. Seated on the chair was a very smart, pleasant looking lady. I would have guessed she was about 38 or 39 years of age. Standing next to this lady was a younger lady, probably more of a girl of about 15 years old rather than a young lady. The strange thing about seeing the two ladies, one sitting and the other one standing, by the side of the bed that I was lying on was that they both appeared vaguely familiar to me as I looked at their features. I just couldn't, at that moment in time, place where I might have seen them.

Of course, when I saw the two ladies there, I put both of my hands up to my eyes and tried to rub them so that I could make out a bit clearer if what I was seeing was true. Just as I lowered my hands from my eyes the lady sitting down looked at me and said, "Hello Stuart, you're with us at last. This young lady standing by my side is Leanne and she's just here to experience how and what I say to you because you've only just joined us, my name is Rita".

I hadn't got the faintest idea what this lady was talking about and so I had to say to her, "I'm really sorry, but I have no idea where I am, who you are and what you could possibly have to say to me."

One of the ladies spoke to me, "No Stuart, I know that, and I also understand that at the moment you have no idea where you are, why I'm here and what I am here to talk to you about. But I must say to you now that what I am about to explain to you is so important that I will have to go through it very slowly so that you completely understand what's happening, and of course you can ask me any question you care to at any time.

It all seemed so strange to me that I was starting to think that it was all top secret and that I was just about to be briefed on some important mission that I knew nothing about. I looked at Rita and decided that the only way I was going to find anything out was to politely suggest that she ought to start to explain to me what was going on.

I looked at Rita quite sheepishly and said, "Well Rita I'm really quite confused with regards as to what is going on, so if you care to explain it to me I will listen with great interest." "Right Stuart," she replied," Do you recall walking down the high street in Potterford making your way to the travel agents to enquire about a cruise to Hawaii for yourself and Nathalie." "Yes of course I do," I replied. It was as if I had suddenly woken up from a very bad dream". "Oh" Rita said, "Then do you remember that there was scaffolding on the front of the travel agents because they were repairing the roof". I had no idea Rita knew all about this, but of course I do recall it quite clearly. I had decided not to interrupt Rita, I would just let her continue explaining the events that had occurred. Rita could see from my body language that I had nothing to say at the moment and so she continued.

"Well" she said, "just as you reached the travel agents you noticed an old man crossing the road whilst using a Zimmer frame. You noticed that he was, with great difficulty, trying to hurry up because the lights on the crossing had changed to green and the traffic was ready to move off but couldn't because the old man was in the way. You had just reached out to grab hold of the Zimmer frame when everything went blank."

"Now Stuart, this is where I start explaining things of which you will have no knowledge, but I want you to take all the information I give to you in very calmly, just as you have so far." To be quite honest I had no idea what Rita was about to tell me and so it wasn't very difficult to remain calm. Very discreetly I took in a large gulp of air and relaxed, I waited for her to start explaining. It seemed as though it was taking her ages to begin, but of course in reality it was just a few seconds and she began.

"As you know there were some men working on the scaffolding just above the pedestrian crossing where the old man was crossing the road. Just at the moment you reached your hand out to grab hold of the Zimmer frame one of the men on the scaffold accidentally dropped two large roof tiles that he was carrying. Both tiles plunged towards the footpath below. Unfortunately, Stuart, both tiles struck you on the head before they reached the ground. One struck you on the top of your head and the other one struck you on the forehead."

"From that instant Stuart, you entered your second phase." At this point I just couldn't understand the last part of Rita's statement, I became so confused I interrupted Rita and said, "I'm sorry Rita but I just don't understand what my second phase is or means, could you possibly explain to me what it means before you go any further." Rita smiled and said "Of course I can Stuart."

Rita began, "Well Stuart when you are born onto the earth, from boyhood you start being taught all about yourself and other human beings on the earth and how you should respect yourself and all others living life on the earth. As you grow older you are educated on all subjects that will become relevant to you. Whatever particular part of the earth you come from you will be taught a religion or a way of life relevant to your particular area. Whatever the different ways are in those areas you are all taught one thing that is exactly the same and that is when you come to the end of your life on earth you die or pass away. But what nobody can possibly know on earth is that you don't die or pass away, the truth is you actually leave phase one of your lives and enter phase two."

"From the instant those two tiles struck you on the head, you entered phase two. Unfortunately, at the moment, all the people who knew you in phase one when you were on earth will believe you have died. But for all of them, at a later date they will discover, as you have, that they don't really die but just pass on to phase two."

Rita paused for a moment, I think she could tell I was processing all this information she had just given me to make sure I completely understood it all. Rita pointed to a shape on the wall, which appeared to be a door, at the same time she looked at me and said," Now Stuart, when you go through that door you should be pleasantly surprised. You will be entering The Hall of Second Greetings. The reason it is called that is because everyone you meet in that room will be someone you knew in phase one when you were on earth. There will be absolutely nobody in the "Hall' that you didn't meet in phase one, even if it was only for a very short while. Of course, you will get to meet for a "Second Greeting" all the people who were close to you, that you thought had died. So, as you can imagine The Hall of Second Greetings is a very happy place to be, and to make it doubly happy you also know that all the friends and loved ones that you thought had died, will be there for you to meet again when they enter their second phase."

"When you enter the Hall, you will be in there for quite a while just wandering around but stopping very regularly to talk to people that you meet who you will remember from phase one. I do have to tell you Stuart, you will very rarely get to talk to more than one person at one time. The reason for this is because a third person might not know who the second person is from when they were in phase one. You will not have to avoid this happening, it just will not happen."

"Of all the things I've mentioned that lies in wait for you when you enter the Hall, is there anything that you're not quite clear about on which you have a question?" I just sat there for a few moments, motionless, and stared at Rita and of course the younger lady standing behind her, Leanne, who for all this time had just stood there with a soft smile on her face. I looked directly into Rita's eyes and said, "Well actually Rita I do have a question, but I don't know if you will be able to answer it for me." In a very friendly manner Rita said," Ok Stuart fire away and we will see." "Well" I said, "I just wandered if there is any way I can know how long I will be in phase two before I move to phase three."

Rita took in a rather large gulp of air and then said, "Stuart that is quite an awkward question to answer, the reason being that when you pass through into The Hall of Second Greetings you will find that time doesn't exist in the same format as you would remember from phase one. You will of course have your own room where you will stay until you feel the desire to return to the Hall again and circulate. When you do go to your room and become non-circulating it's not going to be what in phase one you would call night time. So, putting a time on how long you are going to remain here is definitely an awkward question to answer. I do have to say this to you Stuart, once you have entered the Hall, the thought of moving on will not occur very easily."

"Ok Rita" I said, "Thank you very much for your patience, but there is one last question if I may." Rita smiled again and said, "Of course you may Stuart, ask me anything you wish." "Well" I replied, "When I'm in the Hall will there be anyone to answer questions for me if I have a problem?" "Yes Stuart, if you have a question or a problem you need help with you will find that at regular intervals around the perimeter of the Hall there are doors and on each door you will find a notice saying what can be found inside. The door for a problem to be solved or a question to be answered will be marked "Explanations". If you wish to enter any of the rooms they will just open for you as you approach, if they are vacant." "Ok and thank you very much," I replied, "I don't think there is anything else I can think to ask at the moment."

"All right then Stuart, Leanne and myself are going to leave now, the next time someone comes through the door to see you it will be time for you to enter The Hall of Second Greetings but before you are allowed to go through you will have to perform a small obligatory duty. I don't want to explain what that is now, you will find out in due course."

Chapter 3
My First "Second Greeting"

I had walked towards the door with Rita and Leanne as they were about to leave. We had just reached within a couple of meters from the door when Rita stopped and turned towards me. I could see by her facial expression that she had something on her mind and that she was quite anxious to ask me something. With a rather curios look on her face she said "Stuart, all the time that Leanne and myself have been here, quite often I have noticed a sort of long inquisitive stare coming from you whilst you have been looking at Leanne. I just wondered if you are able to give an explanation for that unusual stare?" "Well Rita" I replied, "Actually there is quite a strange reason for it." I didn't say anymore than that so Rita gave a little smile and said, "Well would you care to share that reason with us?" "Yes, certainly I would. Every time I look at Leanne I'm inclined to think that I've seen her somewhere before." Rita just stared at me without saying a word for what seemed ages. Then she said, "Well Stuart I have spent quite a while explaining to you what happens to you immediately you enter phase two, and that is firstly you will never meet anyone in phase two that you haven't met before and of course that situation has started already and therefore you must realize that you have met Leanne when you were in phase one." I have to admit, although I had been listening quite intently to everything that Rita had explained to me since I arrived in phase two, I was still stunned into silence for a few minutes at what I had just heard. "Really" I said "Then I think the polite thing for me to do is to try and recall where I had previously met Leanne."

I went quiet, Rita went quiet, and Leanne stood there, having never spoken a word since I arrived but now wearing a great big smile, come grin, as she looked at me.

By appearance I would have said Leanne was about 21 years old, now I've got to be quite honest I'm really thinking, how many 21 year old young ladies would I have known, well enough for me to remember now I am 64 years old. After deliberating for quite a while I turned to Rita and said "Rita, the only thought I have that could possibly put me anywhere near remembering a young lady of Leanne's age must be that about 5 years ago at weekends I used to manage the local ladies football team and I'm thinking Leanne must have been one of the players in my team."

Both Rita and Leanne laughed out quite loudly, I felt like a little boy who had got the answer wrong. Rita stopped laughing, but still had a smile on her face and then said "Stuart, it's a good try but I'm afraid it's not correct. What you must remember is, and of course it will be very useful to remember this when you enter the hall, whilst you can see Leanne at about 21 years old, you are seeing her exactly the way she appeared to you the very last time you saw her in phase one. But of course, it's realistic to think that you probably knew her better when she was a few years younger." I stood there saying nothing. I slowly raised my hands, clasped them together and rested them on top of my head. I then started to think, wow, this is getting even more difficult to work out. Then, suddenly, a little bit of logic rushed to my brain. If the young lady, namely Leanne, was younger than 21 when I would have remembered her more easily, then she must have some connection with one of my own children. I dropped my hands from on top of my head, looked both Rita and Leanne quickly in the eyes and then, very confidently said "I think there is a connection between Leanne and one of my daughters, either Anita or Paula." At that point I went very quiet and waited. They both smiled, then after a few seconds, although it seemed like ages, Leanne stepped towards me and held out her hand for me to shake. At the same time, she said, "You're absolutely right

Mr Gifford, I was Anita's best friend when we were both 17 years old, and I will always remember Mrs Gifford and yourself taking me on my first holiday outside of Europe and of course it was with Anita and Paula and we really had the most wonderful time in *Sun City* in South Africa."

As soon as Leanne said that to me the memories just flooded back into my mind. At that time, I remember thinking, although fathers of teenage daughters are not supposed to have these thoughts, I remember thinking, wow she is just such an attractive girl and it was quite obvious that all the guys of her age thought so too. The fact that I was responsible for her safety whilst we were on holiday meant that I had to keep a very close eye on her. The first thing I said was "Leanne, I remember you so well now, and please call me Stuart. What I don't understand is, whilst I remember you very easily from when you were 17, you seem a few years older in appearance at this moment in time and I don't recall seeing you as you appear now." Leanne started replying to me immediately and she did as I requested she called me Stuart. "The reason for you not recognizing me at first is because when you meet someone in phase two, they will always appear how they looked on the last occasion you saw them in phase one. I have to tell you that the last time you saw me in phase one was at Anita's wedding, I think I was 21 years old and you only saw me for a brief moment when I was standing with a crowd of friends from our school days. We both gave a quick wave to each other and that was about it."

"Thanks for explaining that to me Leanne I am starting to understand how it works now. What I don't understand Leanne, is, how are you here in phase one, when you are so young, certainly a great deal younger than myself anyway." "Well Stuart" she replied, "It's rather a shame I'm afraid. You see I got married to Russell when I was 22 years old.

He was a really wonderful man, we were so in love. He was an architect by trade and we enjoyed a very nice lifestyle, and to make life even more wonderful we were blessed with three absolutely gorgeous daughters. Unfortunately, the birth of our third daughter had a few problems. The initial problem was that she was born in the breach position. The biggest problem was, so the experts have said, is that when she was actually being delivered in the breach position, one of her tiny arms that was flailing all over the place, caught hold of one of my main arteries and ripped it open. Apparently, baby Gail was born in very good health. On the other hand, they were unable to do anything about the blood that was gushing from my ripped artery and I immediately moved on to phase two. I suppose the saddest thing is that I never got to see my baby daughter Gail. However, the upside of it all is that I know now that when, eventually, baby Gail arrives in phase two I will get to meet her for the first time, and actually I'm finding that thought quite exciting." Rita stepped forward, "Right Stuart, what about me?" Again, I just stood there for what seemed like ages, and was quite speechless. At the same time I just could not help chuckling to myself. Eventually, even though I was still chuckling away to myself, I said "I'm sorry Rita, what do you mean, what about me?" I really had to control myself now and refrain from bursting into an audible giggle. "Now Stuart" Rita replied, "I'm a little bit disappointed that I've spent all that time explaining phase two for you, you've recognized Leanne but now you're behaving as if you have never seen me before, because you don't seem to recognize me." I was absolutely stunned again. I stood there with my mouth open and I think my bottom jaw had dropped so far down it must have been resting on my chest. After a good while a smile broke out on Rita's face, which then developed into a little giggle. Of course, I didn't think it was amusing in the slightest way, I very nervously said to Rita "Please forgive me Rita, firstly for not recognizing you, and secondly for not acting immediately on the information you have just spent all that time explaining. Once again Rita please pardon me and could you help me to understand why I should recognize you." "Of course, I will Stuart, I'm being a little bit unfair on you, but I'm hoping you see the funny side of it all when I have explained myself." "I'm sure I will Rita, and I just can't wait to hear about it" I replied. "Well Stuart, do you remember when you were nine years old you had to go into hospital and have your tonsils removed." "Yes Rita, I do" I replied. Rita continued, "Well when you regained consciousness from the anesthetic, you were extremely disorientated and I was the nurse sitting at the side of you bed waiting to help you recover."

"Yes!" I exclaimed instantly, 'I do remember you now Rita. I remember at the time, thinking you must be an angel. But Rita, why would you remember me, there must have been many children that you had helped." "Yes Stuart, your quite right." She replied "The reason I remember you is because the day after your initial recovery, when you were almost fully back to your happy, cheerful self, you said to me "I've been very impressed with the way you've looked after me nurse so I've decided that when I'm old enough I shall come back to the hospital and you will be my girlfriend. Stuart, how could I ever forget that day and you?" "I never did come back to the hospital and make you my girlfriend when I was old enough, did I Rita?" "No Stuart you didn't, but I don't think my husband would have been very happy about it so you shouldn't let it worry you." We all laughed at the same time, Rita, Leanne and myself. That joint laughter seemed to bring the topic to an end.

The next thing to be said came from Rita. "It's been lovely for Leanne and myself to talk to you again Stuart but we have to go now, somebody will be along very shortly and you will them be moving on into *The Hall of Second Greetings,* so bye Stuart and don't forget you will know everyone inside *The Hall."* I very quickly had time to say, "Bless you ladies, and thank you." It didn't take long before I started to hear the "silence" it wasn't until this actual moment in time that I had been given a moment to think about what could now be happening back in phase one. My mind was just about to consider that thought when I realized there was a man standing by my side looking down at me as I sat on the edge of the bed. I recognized him immediately it was Mr Cotton who was one of the last tutors I had at university before I achieved my degree. I couldn't help thinking "What the flipping heck could he possibly have to say to me."

Chapter 4
Make your Choice

As soon as Mr Cotton saw that I had noticed he was standing next to me he spoke. "Hello Stuart, how nice to see you after quite a long time. You were one of my best, and I must admit, favourite students, and it's a pleasure to speak to you again."

I wasted no time in replying, "Thank you Mr Cotton, I am actually rather embarrassed about your comments." Mr Cotton jumped in immediately with a reply, "Absolutely no embarrassment is expected Stuart and from now on you call me Allan, this isn't phase one now." I said, "thank you Allan" straight away. It was dawning on me now that in phase two, because you only know people who you had only a convivial relationship with, the atmosphere was always going to be a friendly one, with total equality and respect for everyone you meet.

"Right Stuart, I realise there probably isn't an awful lot we could have much of a conversation about in respect to our relationship in phase one so I'm going to move on quickly and tell you what I am here to speak to you about, ok?" "Oh absolutely, that's fine," I said, starting to feel a bit confused again. Allan then began a fairly long explanation of why he had come to speak to me, well it seemed fairly long but I became so disorientated about what he was about to tell me that I really had no idea what length of time was passing whilst he talked. He began to tell me what it was he had come to talk to me about.

"Well Stuart all I've got to say to you is that the door will open for you and you can then enter The Hall of Second Greetings. But first Stuart you will just have to choose one of the two options I give to you. Everyone who enters the

"Hall" is asked to choose one of two options. Now the choice you have to make is as follows. When you were in phase one Stuart I'm sure you would remember Daniel Spencer and Molly Bickers." "Oh my" I exclaimed, I haven't been in phase two very long but the depth of knowledge that is known about me and mentioned to me on various occasions is quite astonishing. For instance, Daniel Spencer who was better known to me as Danny during my latter teenage years was my cousin. I haven't seen Danny for many, many years now and if I tell you that he was just a couple of years younger than myself, probably making him about 60 years old now, will probably give you some idea of how many years it's been. However, Molly is quite the other end of the spectrum. On the day before I had my fatal accident in phase one Molly had celebrated her seventh birthday. The reason I had known Molly in phase one was because she was the youngest child of our very kind and friendly neighbors next door to us since we had been in "Country Cottage". When Allan Cotton had asked me if I remembered Daniel Spencer and Molly Bickers obviously a few seconds had passed before I said, "Definitely I remember both of them very well, but why should that be relevant to me now that I've moved on to phase two?"

Allan continued, "Well now Stuart, it is your duty to now choose either Daniel or Molly. Once you have chosen one of them, you will be given two options of a path of destiny for that chosen person and whichever path of destiny you choose will be the path of destiny applied to that person forthwith. I can't at this moment explain anything more until you have chosen. Naturally as I am sure you are aware this is an extremely important decision, particularly for the person in phase one that has been chosen. All I can say at the moment Stuart is, this choice of destiny has to be made by everyone before they are allowed into phase two."

How am I going to possibly make a choice between Daniel and Molly, when they both played a huge part of my life in phase one. Firstly, Daniel and I were the very best of mates when we were in our late teens, at that time the fact that we were cousins really was not an important factor to either of us. We really started to become good pals when we both started to play football for a small local team on a Sunday morning. That was when Danny was 15 years old and I was 17. The natural progression of our friendship carried on into the following years and developed so that when we were dating girls we always tried as much as possible to make foursomes.

A few years after we started playing football we decided that we would take our first holiday together, probably Ibiza or somewhere similar. Daniel was 18 at the time I was just coming up to 20. At that time in our lives we were both inclined to be a little bit non-conventional. Neither of us wanted to book what was termed a normal package holiday, so we decided that we would buy an airline ticket to some destination but not to make any arrangements to return home until basically we'd had enough of where we were. Looking back now, it may not have been the wisest decision we'd ever made. At the time, we would discuss how it would all go and usually end up rolling all over the place with laughter after saying things like, we might meet two fantastic girls who lived locally and they were so hot we would end up staying there for about 3 months. Well we hadn't booked return tickets so it wouldn't matter to anyone would it. Of course, that was completely wrong, particularly for Daniel. Daniel was training to be a solicitor's secretary and the practice he was training at was very small. When he told them at his office what we were planning for our holiday they made it quite clear that under no circumstances could they accept him taking more than 2 weeks leave at the moment. I didn't have the same problem because at that time I was working freelance for a company that supplied carers for the elderly so they only employed me as and when they needed me and if I wasn't available they would just turn to someone else on their books.

Our parents were absolutely fine with it. Because they knew we were together, and they were quite happy, so we decided to just purchase a one-way ticket and go for it.

Now I'm just going to tell you what happened on this holiday, just so that you know what Danny did for me on that holiday and why he was such a fantastic mate.

We got off the airplane in Tenerife at ten o'clock on the Saturday morning and caught a taxi to Santa Cruz straight away, as soon as we arrived in Santa Cruz we set about searching for a place to stay. We had gone in June so we thought it would hopefully be quiet enough for us to find somewhere to stay without too much difficulty. Actually, we were right, we found a small two-bedroom apartment just on the edge of town overlooking a quite rocky part of the coast. We didn't mind that, we found it quite comfortable. There was also a couple of pretty good night clubs nearby so we were all set to go.

After the first week had passed by we were having a great time. We would sun bathe during the day, on the manmade beach that wasn't too far away. In the evenings, after coming off the beach about 8:00pm to 8:30pm we would be in one of the night clubs until the early hours of the morning and then we would be in bed until about midday. Not always sleeping though, if you know what I mean, but we made up for sleep when we were on the beach.

We had a good discussion exactly a week after arriving, on the Saturday, about how long we intended to stay. Now

Danny made it quite clear, that he would stay with me for longer than two weeks if I wanted to, but I knew that if we stayed longer than the two weeks Danny would almost certainly lose his job back home and I knew he really didn't want that to happen. So, I insisted that on the Monday we would go and make sure we had got air tickets home the following Saturday. That's exactly what we did, so everything was settled.

Now without taking too long I'm going to tell you what happened on the following Wednesday before we were going home on the Saturday. We were at our favourite nightclub and it was about 12.15am. We were both sitting on high stools at the bar, each of us with our same favourite drink, which was a brandy and coke. We usually started the evening off by telling each other how we had got on the evening before with whichever girl we had ended up with. Suddenly Danny nudged my arm with his elbow, making me spill some of my brandy, and said "Stuart just look at those two babes on the dance floor." I looked over and couldn't help noticing them immediately. Danny and I were discussing how we could cut in without wanting to appear either too confident or too desperate, when all of a sudden the girls turned to face us, grabbed each other's hand and walked straight over to us. I think both Danny and myself sat there with our mouths hanging open. They stopped within touching distance of us still holding hands, and then the one said to us "Hi guys, my name is Erica, and my sister and I could use a bit of company, is that a problem?" Before Danny and myself had a chance to say a word the other girl, still holding hands, said "Hi guys, my name is Theresa, my sister and I could use a bit of company, is that a problem?" Danny looked at Erica and said, "I'm Danny and I don't think that's too much of a problem at all." Danny then spun around and looked at me. Without hesitation, I turned and looked Theresa directly in the eyes and I slowly said, "Theresa, my name is Stuart and I think you and your sister have got no problem and you've got all the company you need."

From that moment everything went unbelievably brilliant, we spent all the night drinking, chatting and dancing. In fact, it was so brilliant we even got to see to it that the girls arrived home from the night club all safe and sound. Even more brilliant, the girls, in the nature of their truly wonderful Danish culture, that's where they both originated from, invited Danny and myself to stop the night in their two-bedroomed apartment. Of course, Danny and myself didn't take long to decide that it was much too kind an offer to refuse.

At this point I have to remind myself that my story isn't about mine and Danny's girlfriend experiences, although I think I could go on and make another very interesting story about them. But I am going to cut that story short now and just say, we had a fantastic night and arranged to see them the following night in the same nightclub. Unfortunately, that was going to be our last night before making our way back to England.

That last night went just as brilliant as the first one, and of course when they invited us to stay the night at their apartment, we accepted the offer. Danny and I had agreed to meet on the girl's balcony at six o'clock in the morning to make our way back to our apartment. I came out on to the balcony first at just on six o'clock. It was an unusual balcony because it had no fence or balustrade around it and when you stood at the edge you could just look down to the concrete path about five meters below. I was standing quietly on the balcony when I heard the door open and Danny stepped out.

My intention was, to spin around, punch the air and say "Danny, another unforgettable night." The trouble was I didn't do that because as I spun around I put my foot too far back and fell backwards down five meters onto the concrete path below.

Two days later I regained consciousness in the local hospital and found that I had a plaster around a multiple leg fracture and Danny was sitting at the side of my bed. It turns out that Danny rushed to me lying on the concrete path and with the help of Erica and Theresa he managed to maneuver my motionless frame onto his back. Because they were unable, for whatever reason, to get an ambulance to me very quickly, Danny carried me on his back for one and half miles to the nearest hospital.

As soon as I had regained my senses fully I turned to Danny and said, "Danny you've got to get back to England as quick as you can, you know what they said at work about being late back". "Yes," Danny replied, "I remember it quite well, but there's absolutely no way that I shall be sitting on an airplane without you sitting next to me."

By the time the hospital was prepared to allow me to leave the hospital to take a flight home, meant that Danny and I eventually arrived back home ten days later than planned. I'm sure you've guessed, Danny was dismissed instantly when he went back to his office.

Well that's a brief explanation of what type of person my best mate was and still is. How am I supposed to make a choice between Danny and Molly?

Chapter 5
Danny or Molly's Destiny

Now I must tell you about Molly. Obviously because Molly is only 7 years old it would be right to assume she could not have played a huge role in my life up until the accident simply because there hadn't been a lengthy spell of time that we would have spent together. Having said that I have to let you know that Molly was and still is a very special little girl. But naturally, according to someone, every little girl is special, and who would argue with that.

Why are little girls 'so special'? Well I'm sure everyone has got their own valid reason to claim that the little girl they are referring to is very special. I don't know the reasons why all the other little girls are special but I can tell you why, in my opinion, why Molly and probably a lot of other little girls are so special.

When little girls reach the age of 3 or 4 years old there is an event that takes place that alters the whole outlook of how little girls view everyday life. What is this amazing event, well as everyone knows when little girls get to be around 3 or 4 years old they eventually find their Mothers high heeled shoes and a handbag. Once these items have been discovered they must be given an immediate test run. Of course, although the high heels clump and clop across the floor as far as the little girls are concerned they fit absolutely perfectly and the handbag couldn't have matched any better.

From that moment on the little girl's demeanor and behavior is that of a fully-fledged adult. That moment is internationally known as "The Fitting of The Magic Shoes". Why does this event make little girls so special? Well it's quite simple really, as soon as the magic shoes are fitted the children suddenly become this wonderful grown up person, but of course they still have "The Innocence of a Child" that's why they are, 'So Special'.

Not long after Molly's parents moved into the cottage next door to ours Nathalie was in the garden talking to Molly's Mum over the garden fence. Molly was standing holding her scooter next to her Mum. She was listening to the conversation as little girls do. I walked up to them and said, "Excuse me for interrupting ladies, I just thought I'd let you know Nathalie, I'm just going to have a quick change of clothes and pop into town for a short while, I hope you don't mind?" "Of course not Stuart, you carry on, I've got plenty of little jobs I need to get done." "I proceeded by going into the house and having a quick shower and putting some clean clothes on. I didn't think I needed to go out into the garden and say that I was ready to go into town because I had already explained my plans so I carried on and went out of the front door. I had just reached the little gate that opened out onto the lane that passed the front of our cottage. I was about to open the gate when a young girls voice said, "Oh Stuart I'm so sorry to trouble you but could I have a quick word with you before you leave?" I knew without even looking up whose voice it was and so I immediately replied, "Of course you can Molly, you know I've always got time to listen to whatever you've got to say to me."

Dropping her scooter to the ground she put both of her hands on her hips and said, "Well Stuart I've just had an important chat with my Mum and Nathalie and explained that whilst they are both so busy doing their little jobs the best thing I could do would be to accompany you into town. I made it quite clear to my Mum that whenever or wherever I was, that if I was with you, I would be perfectly safe. I think they both completely understood and their decision was that if you agreed to take on the responsibility they would be quite happy. So, what do you say Stuart?" I was absolutely stunned! This seven-year-old girl had made all these plans, explained them all to the adults involved and was now standing in front of me, still with her hands on her hips and looking up into my eyes, waiting for my answer as if it was one adult to another. How could this situation ever have taken place? Well the answer to that was quite simple, it was those "Magic Shoes".

I obviously had to make a very quick decision. I let a big smile spread across my face, at the same time I said to Molly, "It would be an absolute pleasure for me to accompany you anywhere at any time Molly." Molly wasted no time giving her reply to me, "Ok Stuart that's settled then, I'll just go and let Mummy and Nathalie know that you've agreed and then we will set off for town immediately." From that day onwards, I have been to Molly everything a friend could be: a guardian, a minder, a chauffeur, an advisor and of course summing all those things up makes me a very close confidante and personal assistant. It was just the most fantastic friendship.

The time had come, I've got to make a final decision, Danny or Molly. I immediately turned and looked at Allan, it seemed like ages since he had given me the two names but of course it was only a few seconds. "I've made my choice Allan, it's going to be Molly." Without any hesitation whatsoever Allan gave me the two choices of destination for Molly, he then said to me "Choose one Stuart." The choices were, she could become one of the most adored, iconic pop singers the world has ever known and be introduced to Kings, Queens, Presidents, Prime Ministers and Heads of State from all around the world. Sadly, when her fame starts to lessen at the age of 30 she will meet her end by taking an overdose of illegal substances. Or choice number two is, she will become a pillar of the local community achieving the position of 'Head Librarian' in the town's main library and she will campaign tirelessly to protect the green belt that surrounds your village and the town. She will go on to become more successful in this project than anyone else has ever been. Her time in phase one will finish very peacefully when she reaches 92 years old.

I made no hesitation at all, I looked straight at Allan and said, "Without question my choice for Molly is the second option." It would be inconceivable that I could possibly condemn Molly to the degenerative end mentioned in option one. Allan quickly wrote something in his notebook, he then hid the notebook out of sight. He looked at me and said, "That's it then Stuart, you can now walk towards that door on the far wall", he pointed towards it as he said it, "When you are quite near to it the door will open. You can then walk through and you will have entered phase two, and the "Hall of Second Greetings."

Chapter 6
The Joy of Phase Two.

Just as Alan had said, when I was about two meters from the doorway, the door automatically opened without me having to do anything to help it. It gently opened towards me and it didn't stop opening until it was at 90 degrees to the wall, thus allowing me a very easy exit into the "Hall".

I stepped through the doorway very slowly, almost as if I had a feeling that I shouldn't be there. The first thing I noticed, once I was in the room, was that the room was, as was the one I regained consciousness in, very, very light, but there were no windows or any other apertures to show where the light was coming from.

I looked around, although the room was very light all I could see were rough outlines of people's body shapes, but I was unable to make out any features to make the shapes distinguishable. I suddenly thought about what I had been told when I was in my room. That was, that everyone in the "Hall" would be someone I had previously been friendly with in some way when I was in phase one. That must be it I thought, you had to think of someone you could remember from phase one and presumably you would somehow come into contact with them.

Naturally you would expect the first memory to be hanging in there, waiting for you to bring it to light would be your mother. Just as I was considering that thought I noticed someone just standing alongside me, gently a warm, soft hand gripped my right forearm. I twisted around to look, "Oh no!" I exclaimed "Oh no!" There, with that oh so memorable beautiful smile and those wonderful twinkling blue eyes, was mother, oh mother it really is you. She held her arms wide open and at the same time she said, "It certainly is my darling Stuart, now you just come here and let me give you a huge hug." There was no way that I was going to deny mothers request. I stepped forward and she enveloped me in her arms and squeezed me towards her bosom so tightly that I could just about take a breath of air. I just stood there for quite a few minutes and didn't even try to move. Within a few seconds of mother taking me into that hug I felt tears trickle down both my cheeks and into my mouth. Mother was hugging me so tightly that I could feel her heart beating so clearly, just as I was able to when I was a young boy, I could almost count the beats. I took a step back, and with tears still trickling down my cheeks I said, "Mother I have missed you so much." Mother raised her hand to my cheeks and with a soft white handkerchief she dried the tears on my cheeks. She then started to say, still with that warm smile on her face and those lovely blue eyes twinkling, "Darling Stuart of course I have missed you. The wonderful thing about being in phase two is whoever you have loved dearly or even just had a friendly acquaintance with in phase one, you will definitely meet them again when they arrive in phase two."

"Right Stuart", mother suddenly said, grabbing my hand, "We are going to sit together on this bench over here, and have a really good catch up." I was starting to get the idea of what was happening to me, it made me feel a bit more relaxed and I was able to start talking to my mother in the same way that I used to when we were in phase one together all those years ago. "Ok mum" I said, "Let's sit on this bench here." We sat down on the bench; I sat there in a slightly leaning forward position with my hands clasped together in a sort of praying action. Mother sat right up close to me with her right hand resting on my forearm and her left hand just at the base of my skull sort of curling my hair with her finger just as she used to do when I was a young boy.

Of course, there was so much that we talked about. It varied talking about different memories we both could recall from the days in our lives when we were both living the past life we had enjoyed in phase one. There was also such a lot of questions from mother about all the different things that had happened to all the family members, and of course quite a number of close family friends since the time she had left phase one and now, in phase two. Now normally the way I remember it was, that talking about dear loved ones and close friends after they had departed from phase one was always a very sad and somber experience. But now I had the enlightenment of phase two, talking about those ordeals had become a much less stressful experience.

It seemed as though mother and I had been sitting there for an eternity talking about so many different things and of course, mostly different people. I was beginning to think maybe phase two means that I am just going to sit here forever. Just as that thought came into my head I said to mother, "Mum, we've talked about so many different people over such a long period of time, although I am truly, thoroughly enjoying myself, does it mean that we will both now just sit here forever, talking about the past?" Mother gave a gentle chuckle and said, "No my darling Stuart, it means that at this moment in time we have talked to each other for long enough. So, what we do now is stand up, say our farewells and walk away in opposite directions." I looked at mother and quickly exclaimed, "Does that mean I will not get to speak to you again." My mother put both her arms around me again and hugged me just as tightly as she had done before, at the same time she spoke gently into my ear, just as she always had done in phase one, and said, "Of course not my darling Stuart, how it works is that if your thoughts should say to you, that you would like to meet with me again and the thought in your mind is strong enough, it will automatically trigger the same thought in my mind. If the thought of us meeting again is strong enough to reach a certain level then we will just come face to face again in exactly the same way that we did this time. That's how it works in phase two, and whoever you meet in phase two will be arrived at in that same manner, and if the thoughts are strong enough in both persons to reach the required level you can meet the same people over and over again." I leant back from my mother's hug and looked her directly in the eyes, I had a huge smile on my face, and said, "Wow mother, that means when everyone passes through to phase two, life becomes Virtual Utopia. "No Stuart", she replied, "It's not Virtual Utopia, its Utopia in reality."

The discovery of how joyous life is in phase two, prompted me to ask what I thought was an ordinary question. "Well mother does every single person who lives through their life in phase one eventually pass through into phase two?" Mother paused and looked into my eyes with what I can only describe as a very deep blankness. She suddenly grabbed hold of my hand squeezed it hard and lovingly and then with a rather serious expression on her face she said to me, "My dearest son, I have always tried to answer any question you have asked me ever since you were a baby boy. Sadly, on this occasion I am unable to even make any attempt to answer that particular question." "Oh, really mother" I replied, "There must be a reason for that." "Yes, my darling Stuart there is, here in phase two there are certain topics and subjects that we are not allowed to discuss amongst ourselves. Whenever you mention one of these topics or subjects to anyone in here they will automatically point to that door over there." Mother was pointing over my shoulder to a door on the far side behind me. I turned and looked I could read the notice on the door which said, "Office for Unanswered Questions". As I turned and looked at mother again she immediately said, "You are allowed to enter that office at any time and discuss topics and subjects that are not allowed to be discussed out here." I stepped forward again to give mother a big hug and to say thank you very much for telling me. Mothers face burst into that glorious smile again and she said, "Right my darling boy, we are now going to separate company for a short while because I know you need a little bit of a change." "Ok mother" I replied I gave her another huge farewell hug and we both slowly walked off in opposite directions. I felt tears well up inside my eyes again, I didn't look back but I just called out, "See you soon mother."

I had turned in a complete semi-circle and was now walking directly towards the door that mother had pointed out to me, "The Office for Unanswered Questions." My walking pace slowed down a little as I headed towards it. My mind was now becoming quite curious to know what it meant and what would happen if I were to make an attempt at entering the office door and ask the question that mother said she was unable to answer. When I had got to within a few meters from the doors I stopped, I clasped my hands together at the back of my head. I spent a short while contemplating the thoughts that were passing through my mind at that moment in time.

Of course, the most prevalent thought was that since arriving in phase two it has been exactly as I was told it would be, so far anyway, and that is I would never meet anyone whom I hadn't known in phase one. My mind then screamed to myself inside my head, "Who could there possibly be inside the Office of Unanswered Questions that I had known in phase one?"

Well, to be honest with you, the thought now of finding out who could possibly be in there that I had known before suddenly became more of an important question to know the answer to than the original question I had asked mother. Naturally there was only one possible choice I could make, I was going in, right there, and then. I put my hands back down at my sides and took another two paces forward, suddenly a message that was in bright green lights appeared across the door. "Please state your name," was the message. "Stuart Gifford", I replied clearly and instantly.

Chapter 7
The Office for Unanswered Questions.

I stood there for a few seconds and waited for something to happen. It did, the message on the door disappeared and another message appeared on the door in red lights, "you may enter." I stepped forward and the door opened on its own without me having to do anything. I walked on and through the door, as soon as I had completely entered the room the door then closed automatically without me having to do anything.

I glanced around the room to see that the fittings were very minimal, in fact there was a desk immediately in front of me, about three meters in distance from me, and a single chair facing each other either side of the desk. Completely encircling the room on the walls at about shoulder height were two books shelves, both completely full of books in various sizes also completely encircling the room. I now should say that the most noticeable thing in the whole of the room was a man standing on the other side of the desk with his back towards me. I wasn't sure if the man that was standing there knew that I had entered the room so I just let out a subdued cough. Immediately a voice spoke out, quite authoritatively but sounding quite friendly "Sit down Stuart and we will have a chat."

I took about four steps forward and sat down on the chair nearest to me. The man turned around and the first thing I noticed was that he was wearing a smart, light grey cloak, that was edged in a bright red braiding all around. The cloak fell neatly from the shoulders, underneath the man was wearing a smart, darker grey suit and a white shirt which was open at the neck. Of course, all that observation only took possibly two or three seconds. Then my observations looked higher to take in the man's facial features. Not for the first time since arriving in phase two was I absolutely stunned. Standing there looking at me with a rather pleasant smile on his face was Mr Edwards. From the age of 11 years until I was 16 years old Mr Edwards was my school headmaster. In quite a relaxed manner Mr Edwards sat in the chair facing me on the other side of the desk, he leaned forward and rested his left arm on the desk, he then held out his right hand directly towards me in an obvious gesture to shake hands. At the same time in what seemed to be a friendly tone he said, "Hello Stuart it really is a pleasure to make your acquaintance again." Of course, I stretched my right hand out immediately I grabbed hold of his hand quite firmly and at the same time replied, "Thank you sir, the pleasure really is mine." There really is one thing about Headmasters and Headmistresses that I think we must all surely agree on, and that is, whatever small amount of contact you've had with them through the whole of your school life, when they do eventually have to speak to you on a one to one basis they always seem to give the impression that they have been your best friend for the whole of your life, how do they manage to do that? Anyway, that's exactly how it was now when Mr Edwards spoke to me. In fact, I recall back in the days in phase one when Mr Edwards was my Headmaster, he only ever spoke to me on a one to one basis on a single occasion. That just happened to be when Mr Ashley, the gym teacher, one lunchtime caught Sonia King and myself on our own in the changing rooms of the gym. He told both Sonia and myself to report to the Headmasters office instantly.

Mr Edwards continued to speak to me in that lifetime friendly way by saying, "Now Stuart please, you don't have to call me sir here in phase two, I am perfectly happy for you to address me by the same name as everyone else does and that is Conrad." It did seem so strange to be talking to a man that I had only once had occasion to come face to face with during my whole time at school, and it felt as if I was talking to my brother.

Mr Edwards, or shall I say Conrad, then continued the conversation between us by saying, "Well Stuart, since my arrival in phase two I've had the opportunity to chat with your Mother on a couple of occasions because we obviously remembered each other from parent, teacher meetings when we were both in phase one. I have to say Stuart I am really pleased to hear how well you've got on and that you have raised a lovely family since leaving school. I can assure you Stuart I'm not in the slightest little bit surprised at all knowing what sort of young man you were whilst at school. Don't let the incident with Sonia bother you in the slightest, all that was happening between you and Sonia at that moment in time was perfectly natural for a young couple of your age's. In fact, I don't really understand even now why the school teaching staff, whenever they encountered these experiences between teenagers, treated them in a manner of shock and horror. Both yourself and Sonia were students that any school would have been proud of. Also, Stuart even though you are now in phase two I have a funny feeling that there is, somehow, still quite a few new experiences ahead of you. Right Stuart, now let's address the business of today, and that is, why have you come to the Office for Unanswered Questions. You obviously, I imagine, have something bothering you, so come right out and tell me about it and I will do my very best to explain."

I had sat there for quite a few minutes listening to everything that had been said and it seemed rather a lot to take in, but of course most of it was complimentary so I was ready to continue the conversation almost immediately. "Well thank you for everything you have said about me Mr Ed----- err, sorry, I mean Conrad, you really have said some very kind things about me. The problem is Conrad, just before I came to this office I had been having a wonderful, fairly lengthy conversation with my Mother when I just happened to ask her a question that she said she wasn't allowed to answer and that I would have to come to this office to find the answer to my question."

Conrad leaned back in his chair outwardly showing that he was quite relaxed. "Ok Stuart, of course your Mother is absolutely right, but first let me explain why. Everyone who comes into phase two is, purely by nature, going to ask a lot of questions and of course there is absolutely nothing wrong with that because it shows the recipient has a thirst for knowledge. What everyone must realize quickly in phase two is that unlike phase one, phase two is non-confrontational, therefore if subjects arise during a conversation that are confrontational, the people holding the discussion must agree that the one who introduced the subject into the conversation must go to The Office for Unanswered Questions to find the answer and the conversation between them must not end until that is done. Now that I've explained that to you Stuart, would you like to ask me the question that became a problem between you and your Mother."

"Certainly Conrad, but first let me thank you very much for explaining that to me so clearly. Now my question was, does everyone in phase one eventually come into phase two?" Conrad stood up and started to pace back and forth for approximately the length of his desk. Then whilst still looking down at his feet and still pacing back and forth he proceeded to answer my question.

"Well Stuart there is a very short and to the point answer to your question and obviously it is a question that many people ask when they arrive in phase two. However, although there is a short and to the point answer, I will have to take a short while after giving you the answer to explain the reason for that answer, so are you quite happy with that Stuart?" "Absolutely Conrad, I've got nothing planned for a short while." Conrad chuckled quite loud enough for me to hear him. He obviously understood the intended humor in my reply. Then he immediately stopped his chuckling and replied, "Right then Stuart the answer is "No" not everyone is allowed into phase two from phase one. Now Stuart before you ask me the next obvious question I am going to explain why."

"Although you haven't been in phase two very long, I'm pretty certain that you already understand that controversy and confrontation have no place in phase two in any form. Therefore, the persons that would never be allowed into phase two are, anyone who, during the whole of their time in phase one had ever intentionally caused or tried to cause the death of another human being. For example, looking back through history certain people who would not have been allowed into phase two would have been, Jack the Ripper, Charles Manson, Fred West, Adolf Hitler, Moira Hindley and of course many more. Don't forget though Stuart, these are only a few famous or should I say infamous people from history, the rule also applies to anyone who causes the demise of another human being. Sadly, Stuart, the rule also includes Euthanasia and suicide."

"I hope that has answered your question Stuart but there is one more "rule". Well I think you would call it a rule and it is necessary for me to tell you about it. Under no circumstances must you discuss anything that you hear about in this room when you leave. Now just to save you coming back to ask me the next question, because I already know what the next question will be that you are about to ask me. The answer is, if you attempt to discuss any topic you have asked a question about in The Office for Unanswered Questions, whoever it is, will be automatically deleted from phase two and will never be spoken of again. Ok, if you have no other questions Stuart that's it but you must remember that you are welcome back at any time if there is anything else that might puzzle you."

I stood up and held out my right hand to shake Conrad's. Conrad gripped my hand very firmly and immediately said, "Thank you very much Conrad and of course I'm sure that I shall be talking to you again."

Chapter 8
Back with Sonia Again.

I stepped out of the office and back into the Hall of Second Greetings, I heard the door behind me click as it shut behind me. In just the few days I had been in phase two I had noticed that the days seemed to float into each other without you really noticing the change. I must admit though I don't know how long I was listening to Conrad helping me out with all the information he gave me, I really did feel now that I just wanted to return to my room and take in some much-needed relaxation.

I got back to my room without meeting anyone else, I went into my room immediately, walked over to my bed and lay back with my head resting very comfortably on my pillow.

As I lay there thinking about the events of the day I thought how strange it was that because my acquaintance with Mr Edwards had been renewed after all these years it had introduced a thought into my mind that probably would never have occurred, and that is "Sonia King", but of course as most people would guess, at this moment in time, the thought that was now completely dominating everything was my meeting with Sonia that day in the school changing room. It also just happened that we were both 16 years old at the time and it was also quite near to the end of our time final term in the sixth form. We both moved on at the end of the term and our paths were never destined to cross again so the experience in the changing room had been our only encounter. I just lay there on my bed and all I could think about was every single move that took place that day.

As I said I really needed to relax and I did drift into sleep and I slept for quite some time. I woke up refreshed and with nothing specifically entering my thoughts I decided to step out of my room into the hall, take a gentle stroll and see if anything happened. I walked for about ten or fifteen minutes when I suddenly came across a bench situated just at the side of the path, I decided to sit down and once again have a little relax. I had just started to drift into some sort of day dream, which I have no memory at all of what it was about, when almost as if I was supposed to be startled a voice to my left said, "Hi Stuart, it's fantastic to see you, how are you?" I twisted around and looked up to see who was speaking to me. I was taken by surprise so much that I said out loud, "No I don't believe it, I just don't believe it, Sonia, Sonia King." As I said it I stood up facing her, she at the same time stepped forward, put her arms around me and hugged me, then in one continuing movement she took both my hands in her hands, stepped back and as she held our hands at arm's length she looked me up and down and said, "Yep, just how I remembered you Stuart." Well of course Sonia was seeing me when I was sixteen and that was 48 years ago, and of course I was seeing Sonia as she was when she was sixteen, which was obviously 48 years ago as well. The funniest thing was that Sonia was also wearing virtually the same clothes that she was wearing in the changing rooms that day, a pair of tight fitting shorts and a tee shirt that had a message on the front saying, "just let it happen."

I looked into Sonia's gorgeous blue eyes and said, "Wow Sonia you look absolutely terrific, let's sit on this bench and talk." Sonia smiled and replied, "Well Stuart, you're looking pretty good yourself so yeah, let's talk." I started the conversation off by asking Sonia how she already came to be in phase two, and how long she had been here. "Well Stuart," she replied, "I've actually been here 22years, I was only 42 years old when I came here from phase one." "Oh my" I gasped, "Who could possibly have chosen that destiny for you, it seems rather cruel?" Sonia looked at me in quite a relaxed manner and said, "Well at first I thought the same, but I spent a considerable amount of time just after I had arrived here in the room of "Explanations" and the "Room for Unanswered Questions" trying to find out who had chosen my destiny and why they had decided I should come to phase two at a relatively young age. I found out, eventually, that it was my aunty Lola. Now I have to say, when I found out the two options she had to choose from for me, I was in total agreement with the one she chose, so it wasn't a problem." I didn't wait a second to say, "Come on then Sonia you've got to tell me the two options you were given to choose from please." Sonia replied straight away, "Ok, the choice that she chose for me was that I would become a professional Ballet dancer, but when I reached the age of 42 I would meet with a fatal accident whilst on stage and that would be the end. The other option was I would become a well-respected barrister's assistant and I would eventually suffer from cancer and move on to phase two when I was 76 years old. Well I can tell you Stuart I was, and still am perfectly happy with the choice my aunty Lola made." "Ok" I replied, "What happened exactly when you met with your accident on stage." "Well", she said "I was dancing the lead role in the ballet "Nutcracker" with the male lead role, an absolutely super guy named Rodrigues, in Rio, Brazil. We were dancing to a sad part of the ballet together when apparently for some unknown reason a large heavy beam that should have been secured quite safely above the stage, somehow came loose and plummeted down to the stage. Unfortunately, the beam, on its way down, struck an instantly fatal blow to myself and Rodrigues."

Sonia and I spent quite some time telling each other about our lives and experiences since our last meeting in the gymnasium all those years ago. Suddenly Sonia stood up in front of me, she had her legs slightly apart and both her hands on her hips, she then looked me in the eyes, gave me a big smile and said something that stunned me for quite a few minutes. "Stuart" she said, "We've now got all the time we need, and the complete freedom we need, to continue from where we were forced to stop that day in the changing room." I sat there looking up at Sonia and then said, "I'm not quite sure what you mean Sonia".

Sonia wasted no time in explaining the situation just as it was when the gym teacher walked in. "Stand up Stuart and face me just the same as we were that day." I stood up slowly, then she continued, "Now if I remember correctly I had removed my tee shirt." She quickly pulled her tee shirt up over her head and dropped in on the floor. For some reason, I never had a chance to find out why she was wearing no bra, her gorgeous sixteen-year-old breasts that were quite firm, with nipples that were quite hard, just bobbled and then rested. Then Sonia stepped forward and started to unbutton my shirt, at the same time saying. "I'll help you with this Stuart because you weren't wearing anything on top either were you?" She helped me off with my shirt and dropped it on the floor alongside hers. She took a step backwards before saying, "Now Stuart, do you remember I wasn't wearing shorts either?" She immediately undid the button and the zip on her shorts and let them drop around her ankles. She stood in front of me in a very brief pair of white panties that had a little bit of frilly net around the waist band and the edge of the legs. Sonia was sixteen but I could tell that she probably only trimmed her pubic hair either when she was going on holiday or swimming. Now, she obviously wasn't doing either because on the inside of the leg area I could quite clearly see tufts of reddish hair protruding from her panties, and the dark shadow showed that for a sixteen-year-old, she had already got a large bush of pubic hair.

Sonia stood there, smiling at me again, then she said, "Ok Stuart, if I remember correctly you hadn't got your shorts on either." Without hesitation, she took a step forward, undid the buckle on my belt, slid my zip down and let my shorts fall around my feet. Without taking a step back, Sonia looked up into my eyes and said, "Now this is exactly how we were in the gym." She looked down and then back up into my eyes and said, "Well Stuart, I think you must be a little bit excited because there's quite a bulge showing at the front of your boxer shorts." I looked down at the bulge she was looking at and sort of tried to brush it away with my hand, but of course that didn't make the slightest difference to the size of the bulge, at the same time I said to Sonia, "Well you know, I think perhaps your somewhat excited because I can see that your nipples are really quite hard." Sonia automatically took each one of her nipples with her fingers and gave them a good squeeze. At the same time, she looked up at Stuart, smiled and said, "Stuart there's something I need to tell you but if its ok with you could we go to your room so that I can tell you there?" Stuart thought, well that seems quite a reasonable request so he wasted no time in replying, "Of course we can Sonia, we'll go there right away." They both grabbed the few items of clothes on the floor, Sonia took hold of Stuart's hand and off they went to his room.

Chapter 9
The Privacy of Stuart's Room

Stuart gently closed the door behind them, they had arrived back at Stuart's room and they were both wearing the same as they were when the decision to return to the room was made. That is, Stuart was only wearing his boxer shorts, with the rather large bulge at the front, and Sonia was just wearing her white panties and her nipples were still hard.

Stuart turned to Sonia and said, "Right Sonia we're here, so I hope you are feeling a little more comfortable." Sonia smiled at Stuart again and replied, "Oh I'm feeling very comfortable now and I feel I can answer your questions about me, perhaps reacting a little bit excited. Well the truth is Stuart, since I left school, quite a few years ago now, I have mixed in the circles of the ballet-dancing world. During that time, I have earned the honourable nickname of "Big Nips". The reason for that particular nickname is because I am particularly well known for having big, hard nipples, and not always associated with me feeling excited. Frankly Stu if you really would like to know if I'm feeling excited at seeing you in your boxers with a bulge at the front, your, going to have to find out by different means, but Stuart, I really don't mind at all if you would like to find out, all you have to do is say "yes or no".

Stuart showed his excitement again and Sonia could tell, Stuart didn't wait a second to reply, "Oh yes Sonia, I would definitely like to know how excited you are, yes definitely." "Ok then Stuart I want you to do exactly what I tell you, right," she replied. "Yes, whatever you say Sonia anything, no problem at all." "Right then Stuart, stand as close as you can, behind me, facing the same direction as myself." Stuart didn't say a word, he just stepped immediately behind Sonia as close as he could without actually making any contact with her, he looked slightly downwards at the back of her neck and said, "Ok". Sonia instantly took a step backwards so that the bugle in Stuarts shorts pressed into the crack of her bottom. Stuart automatically let out an exclamation in the form of a grunt "Ugh". The bulge in his boxer shorts suddenly burst into a full-blown erection with such force that it nudged Sonia a step forward. Sonia looked back over her shoulder and said, "Wow Stuart, are you ok?" She was smiling directly at him as she said it. Stuart stuttered his reply to Sonia, "Err yeah, sure Sonia I'm fine."

"Good" she replied, "This is what you have to do now. Put both of your hands on my hips." Stuart complied with her request and from that moment he followed her instructions without question. "Now" she said "I want you to slide your right hand, slowly, down the front of my groin and into my panties. Keep going, keep sliding your hand downwards so that your fingers go all the way down through my pubic hair. When you reach the point where my groin starts to slope under towards my bottom I want you to let your two main index fingers slide into my pubic lips," At this moment Stuart's cock had become so erect that it was actually aching.

Sonia then let her head fall back onto Stuart's shoulder, at the same time she whispered, just loud enough for him to hear, "Take your fingers out now Stuart and tell me if you notice anything." Stuart immediately took his fingers out and said, "Sonia your pussy is very moist and juicy." Sonia, without hesitation whispered over her shoulder again, "Right Stuart, that is how you know that I am a little bit excited." At this point Stuart wasted no time in taking advantage of the situation. "Ok Sonia," he whispered back "I think I had better take your panties off." Sonia mumbled very quietly, "Yes ok". Stuart put both his hands back on her waist he then slid her panties over her hips and let them fall down around her ankles. He then placed his left hand onto her hip and inserted the two main forefingers of his right hand into her pubic lips. Without letting any time pass by he whispered into Sonia's ear," Your very, very wet down there now and I think the best thing I can do right now is to use my two fingers and make you come". Sonia replied instantly, "Yes please Stuart I think that would be good."

Stuart slowly started to use his two fingers to rub around her clit in a circular motion, keeping the same motion going he speeded up the circular movement. After a short while he slowed the circular movement down again, then, completely changing the motion he let his two forefingers slide inside her slit, he then continued the same circular movement, a slow and fast rubbing motion inside her slit. Now he added an up and down slow and fast motion as well. Stuart continued doing all these variety of finger motions for as long as Sonia wanted him to. Sonia was clearly enjoying what Stuart was doing because of the way she was wriggling and letting out muffled sounds of pleasure.

After about four minutes of massaging her clitoris in this way Stuart suddenly felt the cheeks of Sonia's bottom clench against his thighs, then he felt the whole of her body tremble, at the same time she let out a loud groan of pleasure. Stuart knew that Sonia had come. He decided to stop the rubbing motion he had been applying between her legs. Suddenly Sonia stretched both of her hands behind and grabbed hold of the cheeks of Stuart's bottom, at the same time she called out quite loudly, "Stuart please don't stop please carry on rubbing me in the same way that you've just been doing. Stuart speeded up the rubbing motion again. Within about one-minute Sonia's bottom clenched again, she trembled uncontrollably through the whole of her body and again let out the same sigh of pleasure. Stuart thought, "Wow" she must have climaxed again. He once again started to stop rubbing her clitoris. Suddenly Sonia called out again even louder, "No Stuart don't stop rubbing me, please carry on, you can even rub me harder." Stuart obliged, he kept on rubbing her fast and slow but even harder. Within one minute again Sonia clenched her bottom, trembled and let out a louder sigh of pleasure. She relaxed the grip on Stuart's bottom, at the same time she whispered over her shoulder to him, "Stuart I've finished coming now, that was a triple Orgasm and it was amazing."

Sonia, still looking back over her shoulder said, "Ok Stuart, now I'm going to make you come." She then turned away from Stuart and bent completely forward, she reached back between her legs and took a firm grip with her hand of Stuart's very erect cock. Whilst remaining bent over she watched herself rubbing his cock up and down between her legs. Stuart stood there pressed up against her bottom and still gripping her waist with both hands. After about two minutes Sonia suddenly called out, "You ok Stuart," he made no hesitation in replying, "Oh sure Sonia, I'm absolutely fine." After about another minute and a half Sonia could hear Stuart give a little grunt of pleasure, she immediately doubled the speed that she was rubbing his cock and at the same time squeezed it harder. Stuart was now letting out regular grunts of pleasure as Sonia wanked him. Suddenly Stuart felt the ecstatic explosion go down his cock, he gave out a loud groan as the ecstasy reached the end of his cock and he came over Sonia's arm. Sonia released her grip on his cock, stood up straight and turned around to face Stuart. She took a step forward put her arms around his waist and pressed herself against him. She looked up into his eyes and with a big smile on her face she said, "I think that when you came that was a really good feeling for you Stuart." Stuart smiled back, put his arms around her and pulled her even harder up against him and replied, "It sure was Sonia, thanks to you it was fantastic." They stood there for a couple of minutes just hugging each other, then Sonia looked up into his eyes and said, "I'm glad you enjoyed it, if you would like to kiss me now Stuart I think that would just finish it all off quite nicely, don't you?" Stuart didn't hesitate, he bent his head down slightly and kissed her full on the lips with his mouth open, his tongue wasted no time in exploring the wetness inside her mouth. Of course, Sonia wasted no time in letting her tongue reciprocate. It was a very passionate kiss, it lasted for several minutes, eventually they both leaned back from each other with a smile on their faces to say that they were very pleased with each other.

Sonia broke the silence, "Well Stuart I think we are both pretty well spent and the best thing the both of us can do at this moment is to lie on your bed side by side and have a good few minutes rest and recover some energy." Stuart instantly scooped Sonia up into a cradled position in his arms, walked over to the bed and laid her down. Of course, Sonia was still totally naked and as tempting as she looked to him, and he thought that he might, he didn't he just said, "Good idea my darling you just lie there and have a nice rest."

Chapter 10
The Aftermath

By the time Stuart had walked around the bed and lay down Sonia was fast asleep. Stuart stretched, put his hands behind his head and let himself lower slowly onto his pillow. Before he was ready to slip into the slumber that he was now so looking forward to he decided to let his mind reflect on everything that had just happened between himself and Sonia. The first few seconds he was thinking about it he was feeling quite proud of himself for showing Sonia how "Macho" he could be. All of a sudden, the biggest, darkest cloud ever imagined descended upon Stuart's thoughts.

He kept thinking how could he have let himself become so carried away and do all the things he and Sonia had just been doing. His thoughts were "I am and I have been married to Nathalie for over 30 years and I have two beautiful daughters. I love them all more than anything." Then the absolute worst thought of all came into his mind. "Now that I'm in phase two I know that I am destined to meet them all again eventually. How will I ever be able to face them knowing I have enjoyed what I have just done so much." Stuart sat up on his bed, he had his arms clasped around his knees, which he had drawn tightly up to his stomach, his head was resting on his knees. As he kept on thinking about it over and over again the cloud that was hanging over him just seemed to get darker and darker.

Stuart sat in that position for about twenty minutes after which he started to let out very muffled squeaks of anguish. It was one of these squeaks that caused Sonia to stir, she didn't actually move but her eyes opened, very slowly. What she immediately saw was Stuart with his face buried between his knees. Sonia reached out, rested her hand on

Stuarts thigh and at the same time said quietly, "You ok Stuart?"

Stuart slowly turned his head around and let his eyes meet up with Sonia's. Sonia could tell straight away that his eyes were reflecting the deepest, blankest pool of zero emotion that she had ever seen in anyone, and she had been through quite a few emotional break ups of her own and with friends many times. Sonia suddenly jumped up into a sitting position, she held both of Stuart's hands, which of course were still clasped around his knees, looked straight into Stuart's eyes and said, "Ok my darling I don't want you to say a word, because you need some good helpful advice and an explanation, I am going to give you the explanation right this minute."

Stuart sat there with that deep, blank, emotionless pool in his eyes staring at Sonia. Sonia began, "Right Stuart, I am going to explain. You have to focus, understand and totally, without question, accept that what I am about to tell you is how it is. First of all, at this moment in time you are feeling so guilty about the sexual session we've spent together this afternoon. I know that you've just left a wife and two daughters in phase one, and I know that your guilt is because you love them all very much. But Stuart what you have to understand is that there is no need for the guilt you feel whilst you're here in phase two. You already know that in phase two you will only meet people that you had a friendly relationship with in phase one."

"Although whoever you meet in phase two will be someone you've already met and been a friend of in phase one, it doesn't mean that you will have had a sexual experience with them. Of course, that doesn't mean that you won't meet anyone in phase two that you wouldn't like to have sex with." Stuart raised his head and was just about to raise an objection when Sonia squeezed both of his hands harder and said, "No Stuart don't say anything, you must listen and understand everything that I am telling you." Stuart stayed quiet.

"The important thing to remember is that whenever you meet someone in phase two is that it will always be on a one to one basis and that whatever you choose to do or talk about will stay completely just between the two of you. For instance, if someone had a really hot session that used to work in your office when you were 26 years old and the next day you just happened to meet your wife, the memories of that hot session the day before will not exist in your mind. The only time the memories of that session will exist is when you meet up with the same young woman again, and of course she will only have those memories when she meets up with you again."

"Basically, that means that what I have just explained to you is, that whatever happens at a meeting in phase two stays completely confidential to those two people. Now Stuart I really have tried to explain how it all works in phase two and I'm desperately hoping you understand and that you will stop feeling guilty about our session".

There was silence for a couple of minutes. Stuart slowly raised his head and looked directly into Sonia's eyes, she could see immediately that the deep pools of blankness were gradually but continually starting to show the sparkle of life returning. Stuart began to speak, quite slowly at first, "Ok Sonia thank you very much for going to all that trouble to make me understand." Stuart let a few seconds pass without saying anything. "So, Sonia, does that mean, if I understand correctly, that phase two is life in a world without infidelity." Sonia suddenly threw her arms open wide and at the same time almost screamed out with delight saying, "Stuart darling I love you, you've just summed up everything I've tried to explain to you. Phase Two is a world where in a second life there is no infidelity. Which means there is no such thing as cheating, adultery or going behind someone's back. Therefore, you have no need to feel guilty about anything that happens between you and anyone you meet in phase two. Those meetings will always be, without question, a totally confidential experience."

They were both sitting on the bed crossed legged and facing each other. A cheeky smile began to creep across Stuart's face as he slowly let his eyes look down at Sonia's crotch. At the same time he placed a hand on the inside of each of her thighs and started to let them slide towards her pubic area. Sonia suddenly jumped up and off the bed. "Stuart my darling I love you, we've had a fantastic time today and I think we've both had orgasms as pleasurably as we have ever done before and I'm getting the idea now that you would really like to fuck me."

Stuart looked at Sonia with a fresh twinkle in his eye, but before he had the chance to say anything Sonia continued by saying, "I really have to go now Stuart but I'm sure that because of the way we have both enjoyed ourselves we are absolutely bound to meet up again. So, I would love it Stu if you would kiss me now knowing full well that we will definitely meet again and we will see where that will take us."

Stuart gave Sonia that special smile again, he stood up and stepped towards her, they were both of course still naked. Stuart put both his arms around her, cupped the cheeks of her bottom in his hands and pulled her firmly against his groin. Both their tongues searched frantically inside the others mouth, Stuart started to feel an erection forming in his penis. He wanted to respect Sonia's wishes so he gently took hold of a handful of hair that was hanging down the back of her neck and on to her shoulders. He pulled her back so that her tongue slid out of his mouth, he then gave her a little peck of a kiss on the end of her nose. He loosened her hair, stepped back and said, "Ok sweetheart we will meet again."

They both then put their clothes back on without saying a word. They grabbed hold of each other's hand and stepped towards the door. At the door, they gave each other a kiss that was tender enough for them both to know that their rekindled friendship was nowhere near being over. Sonia hugged him and said, "See you soon darling." Stuart replied, "See you soon sweetheart." The door was opened and Sonia left.

Chapter 11
What Happens Next

The conclusion to those thoughts to Stuart is that life here is the opposite to life in phase one. Meaning that in phase one if you are a good Christian by marrying one woman, raising a family and conduct your life so that you cause no other person harm or reason for sadness intentionally, then that would allow you entry into phase two. Once you have arrived in phase two you are then quite legitimately able to live your life permanently not having to believe in Monogamy.

Stuart walked back towards his bed, he lay down, put his hands behind his head and lay back on his pillow. He stared up at the ceiling and began to think about the events of the day, his first thought was, "Wow did all that really happen." He decided there and then that he needed to give very deep and serious thought about the environment that he had found himself in, and how he was going to accept and accommodate himself to this momentous change to the way of 'Life' he now finds himself in. Yes, 'Life' has to be the correct term for the wellbeing he now finds himself in. He then said to himself out loud, "I know that I've passed on from phase one into phase two, but I still have 'Life'. Today has proved it, I am still able to experience joy, happiness and definitely pleasure. Also of course, if it's true and I have every reason to believe it is, then whatever pleasures I might experience, with whoever I choose, it is not possible for anyone else to ever know."

At that moment Stuart's thoughts again drifted to the events of the day with Sonia. As he thought about those events his mind started to recall days, evenings and nights when he had moments, all different, but just as enjoyable, with many other young ladies that he had spent time with before he had met and married Nathalie. Some of those experiences were pretty hot at times. Just as he started to think about one memorable and unusual experience he had spent with Lucy he started to feel the beginning of an erection again. He quickly took his hands from behind his head turned onto his side and said, "Not now" he closed his eyes and drifted into a relaxing sleep.

Stuart had a much-needed rest, he didn't wake up with a quick jump out of bed as he usually did, his eyes opened very slowly, almost as if he was waking up at the most perfect moment. When his eyes had opened fully he again just lay there, staring up at the ceiling. His thoughts virtually carried on from where he had left off the night before except that he wasn't thinking of Lucy. He was thinking that he now understood how life works in phase two and that the best option he could take was not to question it but to accept it with fully open arms and a very open mind.

With that thought he slid out of bed and went to his shower. Whenever Stuart was in the shower it was always another place he could have a good think. Whilst he was in the shower he began thinking that he was now aware that whoever he was inclined to think about the most would have a good chance of being the person he may well bump into during the day ahead. He began to think he was giving a lot of thought to the very interesting but unfinished session he had spent with Sonia, which of course could lead to a second session taking place today. He was also aware that he had given a lot of thought to quite a few memorable young ladies from phase one, so giving all the thoughts the merit they deserved he decided he would get ready, go out, and just let it happen.

He did one last wipe around his chin with his hand to make sure he was nice and smooth, he opened the door with his other hand and out he went. After yesterday's events, he was feeling pleased and confident with himself as he walked along with a little bounce in his step. Suddenly in just the same way as before he heard a voice call out, "Hi Stuart it's me, how are you?" The voice was coming from over his right shoulder, he turned, immediately he saw a very attractive young lady about 40 meters behind him. She had long ash blonde hair that hung straight down and rested on her shoulders. She wore a gorgeous figure hugging blue silk dress that finished just above the knees. The dress was a deep royal blue color but she was wearing high heeled shoes that were an aqua blue colour.

As Stuart looked back she waved to him, he automatically reciprocated and waved back. The problem was that Stuart had no idea who the young lady was. He started to walk towards her, she continued to walk towards him quite confidently and with probably one of the happiest smiles Stuart had ever seen. As he got closer he started to make out her features in a bit more detail. Her lipstick was a pillar-box red, her eye shadow and her very long finger nails were aqua blue and matched her shoes.

His first thought then was, "Wow she's a pretty smart babe." The trouble was she was getting closer and closer to him but he was still unable to recognize her as anyone he had known from his past. She had now almost reached him, he was getting desperate trying to think of who she was, he even clasped his hands together as if in a praying motion. Just at that moment the young lady reached forward and cupped her hands around Stuart's clasped hands. She looked up into his eyes continued with the radiant smile and said, "Hi Stuart it's me, Nicky, Nicky Clark."

Needless to say, Stuart was still clueless, he stood there with Nicky still holding his clasped hands. After a few seconds, without averting his stare from her sparkling green eyes he began to attempt an apology, "Please forgive me, I know I should recognize you because you're features are so familiar, but you are so beautiful that I think I must remember you from a Miss World Contest that was on the television." Nicky let out a little giggle and gave an immediate reply, "Well thank you Stuart I'm very flattered, of course you know me but I'm afraid it's from a little closer to home. Perhaps I should give you a clue?" For the first time since Nicky had called to him Stuart smiled and said, "Nicky I think that would be a great idea." "Ok" she said, "Your best mate Danny." Stuart automatically realized that there was a connection between himself, Nicky and Danny, who of course he used to hang around with. Stuart looked at Nicky again, "We've met each other when I've been on holiday abroad with Danny?" A quick reply from Nicky was, "No and your next clue is, you both played in the same football team."

Stuart went very quiet, he looked at Nicky's features very closely. Then gradually as if the sun was just rising and making everything visible, he started to place where he had seen those features before. Then suddenly Stuart took a step back, threw his arms open wide and exclaimed "Your Nicky Clark, yes Nicky Clark the physiotherapist from our village football team!"

Chapter 12
Nicky Clark

Stuart composed himself and then calmly, with a pleasant smile on his face said, "Nicky how great to see you again. I can't believe the way I had to stare at you the way I did, before I recognized you." Nicky smiled back and replied, "Well actually Stuart I'm not really surprised that you couldn't make out who I was at first, simply because on all of the many occasions that you saw me in phase one, when I was your physio-therapist, I always wore a grey track suit and trainers." "Yes, Nicky that's absolutely true but look at you now, you look positively stunning." Stuart couldn't help flattering Nicky, but of course Nicky knew that she looked stunning and she had decided to let him know. Well she said, "The first thing I did this morning was go to the room of requisites and acquired these rather hot clothes I'm wearing and the reason is I had a feeling something rather special would be happening today and of course here you are Stuart. I can also tell you Stuart that what I'm wearing underneath, that you are unable to see, is pretty hot as well." Stuart suddenly had a vision in his mind of Nicky standing in front of him just wearing a frilly pair of very skimpy panties with a bulging bra to match and her very hard nipples forming that wonderful titty shape. As regular as clockwork Stuart felt the flicker of an erection forming between his legs. He realized immediately that he had to change the thoughts that were in his mind. "Really Nicky," he mumbled his reply. "What is the room of 'Personnel Requisites' exactly?" Nicky smiled back at him with that warm friendly smile and replied, "Oh I'm sorry Stuart you haven't been in phase two very long have you, I'm sure that there are quite a number of things about phase two that you've yet to find out." She paused before saying, "I know you haven't been here very long because I think we would have met before now. Anyway, the room for 'Personnel

Requisites' is a place that everyone who arrives in phase two should discover as soon as possible, because you can go to there and ask for anything that you might have a need for as long as it isn't anything that could be used in a confrontational manner. It's like 'Amazon' in phase two but you don't have to pay. In fact, Stuart, I have got a number of personal belongings in my room that I've acquired over the years from 'Personnel Requisites', and I absolutely insist that you come to my room with me, we can have a coffee and a really good catch up."

Nicky grabbed hold of Stuart's hand and then virtually forced him into a gentle jog back to her room. She opened the door and they both stepped inside. She was still gripping Stuart's hand, with her other hand she pushed the door shut. Stuart felt straight away that there was a comfortable, homely feel about the atmosphere in the room. It was this feeling that caused him to remember Nicky commenting that he hadn't been in phase two for very long. This of course made him wonder how long Nicky had been there. Just at that moment Stuart noticed that in the corner of the room there was a massage table similar to the one Nicky used at the football club in phase one. He couldn't help letting out, "Wow a massage table." Nicky gave that big smile again and said, "Of course Stuart and we will get to talking about that soon enough, but first of all, you sit down there and I will make coffee." Only a few minutes had passed when Nicky walked over to where Stuart was sitting on the settee, she placed the two coffees on the small rectangular table that was in front of the settee, she then sat down next to Stuart. Stuart said thank you, picked up his mug of coffee and began to drink it. Nicky watched him drink his coffee, at first she didn't say anything, then just as he put his mug back on the coffee table she couldn't hold back any longer. "Stuart, all those years ago when I was your physiotherapist and we knew each other quite well, couldn't you tell how much I fancied you?" Stuart felt himself blush slightly in his face. Nicky had noticed him blush and before he had time to reply she said, "You really don't have to be embarrassed Stuart, I fancied you like crazy then and I still do." She stretched both her arms out, placed a hand on each side of his face pulled him towards her and gave him a rather sensual, lingering kiss on the lips. She leaned back, let her hands slide down his chest and come to rest on his hands, which were just resting on his lap. She didn't say anything, she just sat there looking into his eyes. Stuart could see that the look in her eyes was no ordinary look and it immediately prompted him to say, "Nicky I'm so flattered."

Before he had finished saying flattered, Nicky interrupted him and said, in an almost pleading manner, "Stuart I don't want you to be flattered or embarrassed, I just want you to know without any doubt how crazy I still am for you." Stuart suddenly thought to himself, I am going to have to concede here, then he said, "Ok Nicky, I believe and understand how crazy you are for me." Once again, almost before the words had finished coming from his lips, Nicky blurted out, "Stuart, can we please continue where we left off the last time we met in the physio room all those years ago?" Stuart didn't waste any time replying anymore, he was just going to go with the flow. "Sure," he replied, "But you will have to tell me what happens next." Nicky's face was positively beaming now. "Right" she said, we will have to go over to my massage table. I will prepare it so that you are in a sitting up position. But the last time you were sitting on my massage table Stuart you were only wearing shorts so you had better slip all your clothes off just leaving your boxer shorts or briefs on and jump on to that bed." Stuart realized now that psychologically he had totally conceded to whatever Nicky suggested. He flipped his shoes off then bent down and pushed his socks off. He looked up at Nicky, she stood there, arms folded and with that great big smile on her face. Stuart pulled his shirt over his head, unbuckled his belt and let his trousers fall to the floor, he was left standing there with just the briefest of underpants on. He glanced behind him, put both of his hands on the bed and did a backward jump to finish in a sitting position on the bed. As Nicky walked up to the side of the bed she said, "Well done Stuart, now we are getting somewhere aren't we? It just happens to be a fact that way back when the village football match had finished you were almost always the last player to come and see me in the physio room, that's if you felt that you needed any help. I loved you for it, the reason being that all the other guys who came in for treatment would run and almost fight to see who could get on the bed first, they were always sweaty, smelly and dirty, I used to hate it. Then like I said, you would be the last one and that was because you would always, without fail, go and shower first. I would always make sure that during the gap between the other guys coming in and then you after your shower, I would put fresh clean cotton covers on the bed. I absolutely adored the fresh smell of your body." Nicky pushed the rest down that Stuart was leaning on, and then putting her hand onto the middle of his chest she gently pushed him back so that he was lying down.

"Stuart, when you were lying back on that bed I just fancied you like crazy, I would do little things that I thought might encourage you to ask me out on a date. For instance, I used to do this," she leaned right over the top of him to smooth the sheet down on the other side of the bed, at the same time letting her breast slide across his chest with enough pressure that he couldn't help but notice. Then leaning back up and looking at him she said, "Another move I would make to hopefully encourage you to ask me out was this, I used to scream inside myself to massage your thighs like this." Her very experienced fingers started to brush his thigh muscles downwards from the groin to the knee. Then, whilst still massaging his thigh she said, "What I used to do was, when I brought my hands back up to your groin to press down again I would let my fingers quite deliberately and quite firmly brush your cock like that." Stuart recoiled slightly, at the same time letting out an audible "Oh." Automatically, and true to form, as soon as Nicky's fingers brushed over his cock he started to form an erection. Nicky noticed the swelling instantly, she took a step back, threw her arms open wide and giggled. She turned her head and looked at Stuart directly in the eyes and said, "Fucking great Stuart, all those years ago nothing, but now just a flick of your cock and you get a hard on." Stuart gave her a great big smile.

Nicky put both of her hands on her hips and said, "Right Stuart I'm going to show just how much I still fancy you." She walked back over to the bed told him to sit up and then raised the backrest for him to rest against. She then walked around to the end of the bed and stood facing Stuart, she stood there motionless for a few seconds and then slowly, she stretched her left arm over her shoulder and gripped the top of her dress. Again, very slowly, she stretched her right arm behind her back, took hold of the zip pull and slid the zip right down to the bottom. She then let both her arms fall and hang loosely by her side. Her dress easily slipped off her shoulders and crumpled in a small heap around her feet.

She stood there motionless for quite a few seconds, mainly so that Stuart could enjoy just looking at her wearing just her undies. He obviously noticed that her bra and panties were the same color blue as her dress. The panties had an edging of red lace around Nicky's legs. Her bra was slightly different from the norm, it was the same color blue to match the panties and the dress but there was a hole in each cup to allow her nipples to protrude. Stuart noticed instantly that her nipples were quite swollen and appeared to be quite hard. Just then Nicky spoke, "Now Stuart, would you like me to take my bra off?" Stuart was becoming a bit more relaxed now, he slowly folded his arms and said "Err, well yeah, that sounds like a pretty good idea." Nicky, without a second's hesitation, stretched her arms behind her back and unhooked her bra. She took each strap in her hand and slid them down her arms and cast the bra onto the floor at her side. She didn't put her hands back on her hips at first, instead she slid them up the front of her body from her stomach and slowly over her breast. As soon as her hands had passed over her breast she loosened them and let them bobble back.

Stuart noticed that although Nicky had large breasts they didn't bobble very much because they were very firm. Nicky put her hands back on her hips, and then, still smiling, she spoke again. "Stuart do you want me to take my panties off?" Stuart remained calm and sat there, still with his arms folded, then with a smile on his face he said, "Yeah, that seems a reasonably good idea and I'll sit here and watch you." Nicky, in what seemed to be almost girlish excitement put her hands together and gave a little jump into the air. "Ok" she said, excitedly, "But first Stuart I have to warn you about something." "Oh, what's that sweetheart?" Stuart replied in a very affectionate manner. "Well" she said, pointing between her legs, "I don't shave down there, I hope that doesn't stop you fancying me?" Stuart gave her that big smile again and said, "Not in the slightest my darling."

Chapter 13
Nicky's Fantasy

Nicky placed a thumb in each side of her panties at the hips, gently slid them off and let them fall to the floor, she put her hands back on her hips and said, "I'm all done then Stu, this is me and this is what you get if you want it."

Stuart sat there on the physio bed with his arms folded so tightly that his excitement wouldn't show especially now he could see that neat triangle of black hair at the top of Nicky's legs. That would always guarantee any man would get excited, and of course there was no way that Stuart could hide the excitement that his erection was showing, in fact he was now so hard that his penis was straining to poke its head out of the top of his briefs.

He let his eyesight drift slowly up to look into her radiant face and said, "Wow Nicky, to think what I missed all those years ago, you are absolutely gorgeous." Nicky replied immediately "Thank you Stuart, but you are not going to miss out now because with your permission, I am now going to act out the fantasy that I have been living in my mind, over and over again for all those years. So, Stuart you've just got to say you don't mind and I promise you it is going to happen now."

Stuart decided that now was probably a good time to torment her a little bit. He put his right hand on the end of his chin and sat there for about two or three minutes making it look as though he was thinking about it. "Ok Nicky" he replied, "If you really would like to, I can't really think of any reason why I should object so I'll try and be as co-operative as I can." There were times when Stuart, as nice a person he was, could be deceptively cynical. Nicky gave that little girl jump in the air again, she ran over to Stuart, shouting, "Stuart I love you". When she reached him, she flung both her arms around his shoulders and gave him a very passionate kiss making sure that her tongue went into his month as far as she could get it to.

Nicky didn't waste any time now, she took one step back and lowered the back rest that Stuart had been leaning on. She put both her hands on Stuart's chest and with a little pressure made Stuart lie flat down on his back again. "Right my darling Stuart," she said whilst rubbing the palm of her hands gently together, "I'm going to begin now but to help you Stu, what I will do as we go along is give you a verbal commentary on what should be happening next so that if you think you can assist in any way, it could help it all to turn out successfully, ok?" "Oh absolutely," Stuart replied with a big smile on his face, "I promise I will try to follow your instructions to the letter." Nicky immediately climbed onto the bed and sat down on top of his thighs with her legs straddled either side. Nicky looked down, she could see the head of his very erect penis poking out of the top of his briefs.

Nicky, now with a look on her face that was saying she was ready to start she said to Stuart, "Ok darling I'm going to roll the top of your briefs down a bit and start rubbing your very hard cock. I think it would be good if you could take each of my breast in your hands and caress them so that my nipples become really hard." Stuart looked up into her eyes, smiled and said, "Sure sweetheart, whatever you say." Nicky looked down and rolled back Stuart's briefs. As soon as her eyes started to look up at Stuart he cupped both his hands around Nicky's breasts and started to caress them. Nicky immediately looked back down and started to manipulate Stuart's cock. The manipulation soon turned into one hand gently caressing his balls and the other hand gripped his cock and started to rub it up and down. She gently wriggled herself in a circular motion on the top of his thigh.

Suddenly she squealed out, "Oh gosh," and put both of her hands on the side of her face. In a tone of shock Stuart said, "What sweetheart, what's the matter?" Nicky looked at him and pleadingly replied, "You won't come, until I tell you, will you Stuart?" Stuart looked at her, smiled and said, "No my darling, I promise I won't come until you want me too." Nicky leaned down and gave him long passionate kiss again, making sure that her tongue went as far into his mouth as she could. They both resumed what they were doing, Stuart, caressing and fondling Nicky's breast, and Nicky continued to grip Stuarts cock hard and at the same time working it up and down, Nicky also continued to gently rotate her clitoris on the top of Stuart's thigh.

There was now, for quite a few minutes, silence with both of them very engrossed and presumably enjoying what they were doing. Nicky broke the silence, she stopped rubbing Stuart, looked at him and said, "Right Stuart, you now have to say to me, Nicky I want you to turn around to face the other way and sit down again but a little bit higher so that you are sitting on my tummy." Stuart did exactly what she had asked him to do and Nicky then followed his instruction. As soon as Nicky raised herself from his thigh, Stuart could feel the wetness from her clitoris. She manoeuvered herself around to face his feet and then sat herself down on Stuart's tummy. Stuart immediately put his arms around Nicky and started to caress her breasts and squeeze her nipples again. Nicky carried on rubbing Stuart in the same way as before. It went quiet again but not for very long when Nicky again broke the silence, "Ok Stu, now you tell me to bend all the way forward and rest my cheeks of my face between your knees." Stuart had no idea what the reason for this manoeuver could possibly be but he obediently followed her instructions. Nicky didn't hesitate for a second, when her face was resting between his knees she then said, "Stuart, spank my bottom three, four or as many times as you want to, at the same time you have to say to me, Nicky, that's for being naughty." Stuart automatically thought, even though I'm doing all this to please Nicky every time she asks me to do something I can feel my cock getting harder and harder. Stuart did exactly as she asked, he spanked her bottom about five times quite hard, and told her that she was naughty. As soon as he had stopped spanking her she sat down on his tummy again. He put his hand between her legs and could feel that the wetness had increased considerably.

Nicky then said in a very mild tone, "Why am I naughty Stuart?" Obviously, Stuart didn't know what to say, Nicky immediately followed up by saying, Stuart you must say, "Because Nicky you told me not to come and that's very naughty isn't it?" Stuart said exactly what she had asked him to do and then just waited. Nicky didn't let the silence last many seconds when she said, "Ok my darling I promise to be very good from now on." She immediately started to rub his very erect cock in the same way as before, Stuart continued to caress her breasts. Silence prevailed again whilst they both focused on what they were doing, after about two or three minutes Nicky stopped what she was doing, leaned forward slightly and with her arms outstretched, rested both of her hands on his thighs. As she was resting on him she said, "Now Stuart what you have to do is put your right arm completely around my waist and clasp me in your arm firmly and lift me up so that my bottom is about seven inches above your tummy, then use your left hand to position the head of your cock at the entrance to my vagina and then slowly lower me back down." Stuart didn't make any comment he followed Nicky's instructions totally. As he lowered her onto his cock she let out that all too familiar groan that said, "Oh that feels good." Stuart was so hard and Nicky was so wet that she slid down on him very easily and came to rest on his tummy again. Nicky's instant and natural reaction was to lift herself up and down again, she continued the motion of raising herself up and lowering herself down, on each downward stroke there would be the groan of pleasure. Stuart was now holding her on both sides of her waist and assisting her to lift up and down.

That motion continued for several minutes until suddenly Nicky stopped and said, "Stuart darling I have to turn around so that we can see each other's face, is that ok?" Stuart took his hands off her waist and said, "Of course it is sweetheart whatever you say." Nicky lifted herself up, turned around, and swung one leg over to the other side of him. She raised herself up, grabbed hold of his cock and lowered herself onto it again and continued the up and down motion. It all went very quiet again except for the, "Oh that feels good" from Nicky on the downward strokes. After a couple of minutes Nicky increased the speed of the up and down motion, she went faster and faster. Suddenly she bent right over at an angle and placed her nostrils against Stuart's left ear. She kept going up and down faster and faster but now she was snorting warm air into his ear, this in turn started to make Stuart breath very heavily. Nicky kept that up for about one minute and then whispered loudly into Stuart's ear, "Come Stuart, come now, now Stuart come please." It was like flicking a switch, without containing himself for any seconds whatsoever his whole body stiffened and that explosion of pleasure burst down his penis. At the same moment, he let out the obligatory groan of pleasure that always accompanied the explosion of pleasure. Just as the last groan was leaving Stuart's lips the whole of Nicky's body shuddered, she then let out a loud squeal of delight, her body tried to shrink up into a little ball, she had also reached her orgasm.

Chapter 14
How Lucky Was Nicky

They were both totally spent, Stuart let both of his arms flop onto the bed either side of him. Nicky rolled off him and into a little ball at his side with his right arm curled around her. He stared at the ceiling, at the same time he curled his right arm up and snuggled Nicky right up to his chest. As Nicky snuggled up to his chest she let her right leg swing over and come to rest across Stuart's thighs. Stuart looked down to see Nicky looking up into his eyes. He kissed her on the forehead and said, "Wow sweetheart that was a hot session." Nicky kissed Stuart long and hard on the chest, she lifted herself up, leaned on her left arm and then putting her right hand around Stuart's chin she said, "Darling I've been here in phase two for more years than you could possibly know about and almost every night for all those years I have fantasized about what we have both just experienced and Stuart, my darling man, it all went perfectly."

They both lay there for a few minutes and hugged. Stuart was the first to speak, "Well sweetheart knowing that we've just had that wonderful time together I am thinking that perhaps one of the first things we should have spoken about when we first met each other should have been the chosen destiny that brought us to phase two and ultimately back for a second happening together. I think it would be polite of me to say now Nicky, what was the chosen destiny that brought you to phase two?"

Nicky instinctively brought her hands up and put them over her ears, at the same time whilst shaking her head from side to side she said, "Oh Stuart what a question, oh no." Stuart squeezed her towards him a bit harder saying, "I'm sorry sweetheart I didn't mean to upset you, just forget I even mentioned it." He kissed her on the forehead again and squeezed her even tighter still. Nicky didn't wait too long before speaking again, "The thing is my darling Stuart, I have been in phase two for a much longer period of time than most people would care to think and during all those years, until now, I have avoided answering that particular question by simply manipulating the conversation. But Stuart, my love, at this moment in time I don't think I can deny you a full and truthful answer."

Stuart looked into her eyes and lovingly said, "Sweetheart you do not have to give me any explanation whatsoever, especially if it's going to cause you any distress." "It's ok Stu but I don't want you to feel sorry for me in any way at all because now that I'm here in phase two I'm very happy and everything that I tell you is now in the past of a previous life. I will begin telling you my story my darling, but you have to understand that I know what a very, very lucky girl I am to be in phase two, probably the luckiest person here."

She paused for quite a while, then she looked up so that her eyes met Stuart's and said, "I'm not here because of my chosen destiny." She paused and looked away from Stuart. She then jerked her head back to the same position, looked Stuart in the eyes and slowly but quite loudly said, "I committed suicide." Silence prevailed, after a while Nicky spoke, she spoke a little quieter now, "I know you must be thinking how can you possibly be in phase two when one of the rules that stops you being allowed into phase two is that you must not commit suicide. That's why, as I mentioned earlier, I do know how very, very lucky I am to be here." Stuart was a little bit shocked at what Nicky had just told him and he couldn't think immediately what to say. Nicky carried on with her explanation, "After I had ended my time in phase one on earth I suddenly found myself in that little room where they come and ask you to choose a destiny, I'm sure you remember don't you darling?" "Of course I do sweetheart, I remember it well" was Stuart's reply. Nicky continued "I was sitting in that room, waiting, as you do, about ten minutes later a door opens and in walks my headmistress from my junior school, her name was Miss Potter. She walked right up to me and said, Nicky Clark, you remember me don't you? My reply was as if I was still at school. Oh yes Miss I do remember you." Miss Potter then went on to explain all the rules and expectations you were supposed to comply with before you were accepted into phase two. When she had finished the explanation, she paused. She took Nicky's hands and held them between her hands before delivering the most amazing statement, which was as follow's.

"Well Nicky, normally for someone who has committed suicide, I would have to ask you to stand up and go through that door over there and I'm afraid once you have passed through that door you would never have any experience in phase two. However, your case has been given long and serious consideration by the Judicial Committee because you were so very badly physically and mentally abused in your last three years in phase one they are taking the very unusual step of overlooking your choice of suicide due to the extreme provocation you endured, but you will not be allowed to make the choice of destiny that is normally expected."

Nicky looked up at Stuart again, she had a tear from each eye trickling down each side of her nose as she said to Stuart, "And that's it I'm here with you which can't be bad can it?" Stuart took her up in his arms, hugged her really close to him and said, "Oh sweetheart I really feel for you, I really do. I also think that whatever the abuse was that you had to suffer must have been horrendous. Perhaps it would help if you told me about it?" Nicky lay back down on the bed and went quiet for a long time, she stared at her hands that were clasped together and resting on her tummy. After about three or four minutes of lying there without saying anything she suddenly sat up, put both of her arms around Stuart's chest and hugged herself firmly against him. Then after about another minute of sitting in that position without saying anything she suddenly, without releasing her arms from around his chest and keeping a firm grip on him, she started to mumble some words.

Stuart interrupted and said very gently and very lovingly, "Sweetheart you will have to speak up a bit, I can't make out what it is you're telling me." Nicky immediately started to speak louder. "I was thinking Stuart, that if I did explain to you about it, you will be the first and only person to know why I did it, and why I did it without telling anyone else in phase one, on earth that I had a problem. But of course, I do know that the Judicial Committee here in phase two know all about it, and I'm very grateful that they do. So, my darling I am quite willing for you to be the only person to hear my story but I must warn you it is a pretty grim story. The choice is yours my darling."

Chapter 15
A Grim Experience

Stuart gave Nicky a long kiss on her forehead, he lay back on the bed, held her around her waist and said, "Ok sweetheart I'm going to lie here as if I were your tablet of stone and you can let it all spill out." Nicky lay down and rested her head on his chest. Stuart lifted his right hand and gently stroked her hair as she began her story. "About three years after you had finished having any contact with the football club and I was still the Physio there I met a guy at the club named Andy. We got on really well together and he used to spend a lot of time at the club helping the younger boys to develop their skills. In fact, we got on so well that within six months we were married."

"Of course, everything was great for the first three months and then things started to change. The first one was that Andy insisted that I give up working at the club. He claimed it was a conflict of interest because he was also spending a great deal of time there. In fact, he absolutely insisted that the only place he would allow me to work was the local supermarket on the tills. I objected, but I didn't make too much of a fight about it because we hadn't been married very long and I still loved him. It was just after I started to work at the supermarket that I started to find out what an evil, wicked person he really was. I am going to tell you about the events that started to take place but I really don't want to include all the details because they are too awful. On Tuesday evenings, he would usually come home from the football club at about ten o'clock in the evening after staying there to have a beer with the other guys involved with the club. Around the third Tuesday after I had been working at the supermarket he came home and said that the club had asked him if he would form an evening class on Wednesday evenings to teach the 16-year-old youth trainees some general outside social etiquette. He told me that he had agreed to do it as long as I didn't object. Obviously, I couldn't think of any reason why I should object, in fact I thought it was rather a nice idea so I willingly agreed. The following Tuesday after coming home from having a few beers with the guys he told me he was starting the boys social class the next day and that a few of the lads would be coming around after their dinner and I told him that was fine. The next evening, I arrived home about 6.45pm. As I walked up to the front door I could see four bicycles leaning against the fence. I opened the door and I could immediately hear voices coming from the back lounge so I went in. Sure enough there were four lads sitting together on the L shaped suite. There was a Chaise Lounge facing them about three meters away and Andy was standing just behind it. As I walked in he said, "Hi babe, he always referred to me as "babe" when he wanted to make himself sound big, come in and meet the boys."

"Andy turned to me and said, "Ok babe how would you like to sit on the Chaise Lounge for a while why I explain what's on the curriculum this evening." I sat down and rested back for a while. Andy began to speak to the boys, "Right boys we are going to start your tuition off by teaching you to understand a woman's body which will hopefully be useful to you in the very near future. So now Nicky will stand up in front of you, take off her clothes, and explain what feels good and what she likes done to the various parts of her body. He turned to me and said, "Ok babe stand up and slip out of your clothes." All I could do was stare at him, then without saying a word I stood up, walked out of the room and into the kitchen. Andy hot on my heels followed me. He walked right up to me and said, "You ok babe? Is there a problem." I glared into his eyes, and after a few seconds I said, "Are you fucking serious?

You bet there's a problem, you must be fucking mad." He looked at me and almost apologetically said, "Wait there I will go and send the boys home."

He was gone for quite a long time, I waited there with my arms folded. When he returned he apologized for taking so long but he had to pop into the garage. Then with his hand in the small of my back he started to usher me along whilst saying, "Come on we'll go back into the lounge and have a little chat." When we got back into the lounge he said, "Now, just do as I ask you because if you don't we are never going to sort this problem out." I didn't want to argue with him about it anyway so when he asked me to stand behind one of the single armchairs that was in the room, I did as he asked. Then he said, "Under no circumstances do I want you to move from that spot unless I say so." I felt fear go through the whole of my body. He suddenly bent down and took hold of a piece of rope that was protruding from underneath the chair and immediately tied it around my ankle, before I had chance to gather my thoughts and say anything he took hold of another piece of rope that was protruding from underneath the chair and tied that one around my other ankle. I managed to say, "What the fuck are" when he pushed me and I fell forward over the back of the armchair. He rushed around to the front of the chair, grabbed hold of the other end of the rope that he had tied around my ankle and proceeded to tie it around my wrist in a taught manner so that I was held bent over the back of the chair. He then took hold of the other end of the rope that was tied around my ankle and tied it around my other wrist. He sat down on the floor in front of the chair looked up into my face and said, "Right babe we are now going to sort this problem out and I want you to remember this because if I have to repeat this lesson again I won't be as soft with you."

He stood up, walked around to the back of the chair and stood behind me. I was wearing some body hugging, grey stretch trousers, He put his hands inside the waistband on either side and yanked them down to my ankles. He put one hand inside the waistband of my panties and with one pull tore them off me completely. I could feel my legs and the cheeks of my bottom trembling with fear. He walked back around to the front of the chair and stood right in front of me. All I could see, because I was unable to raise or lower my head, was the buckle to his leather belt, which was directly in front of my eyes. My nose was just pressing against the zipper of his jeans. He slowly raised his hands to the belt and undid the buckle, he slid the belt completely out of the loops around his waist and folded the belt over to form a large loop, he held the buckle and the loose end of the belt together in his right hand. He walked around to the back of the chair again and stood behind me. I could feel the zipper of his jeans again, pressing against the cheeks of my bottom.

I could feel myself start to visibly perspire around my body and on my brow. I heard him step back, I could feel him letting the looped end of the belt brush across the cheeks of my bottom two or three times. He started to speak in a harsh, guttural voice, "Right Nicky, babe, do you know how you have embarrassed me in front of those boys tonight." I had just started to reply with the word "but", when he lashed me across my bottom with his belt so hard that I screamed out loud with pain. He spoke again, "Don't lie to me, do you know how much you embarrassed me in front of those boys." I had just got the "but" out, when he lashed me again as hard as he could, shouting at the same time "Don't lie to me." I screamed in agony again so I decided it was probably best not to say anything. But then he lashed me across my buttocks again shouting, "Oh so you think you can ignore me do you?" He brought the belt down across my buttocks again, and again, and again, after each lashing I would scream out in agony. It didn't make any difference, he kept doing it over and over for about ten minutes.

When he stopped I was draped over the back of the chair like a rag doll. He put his belt back on then bent and released the ropes from my ankles and wrists and started to walk away. As he was just about to leave the room he turned around and shouted, "Don't forget, I don't want to send those boys home disappointed again." After about an hour I managed to get myself to the bathroom, it was then that I could see that the cheeks of my bottom were bleeding quite profusely, they didn't stop bleeding completely until four days had passed. About two weeks later, one Wednesday morning, when I was sitting at the breakfast table, he walked in and said, "Try and get home a little bit earlier tonight because the boys will be coming around to start their tuition again." I immediately glanced over to him, as I did he raised his right hand, smiled and tapped the buckle on his belt four or five times. I diverted my glance away and mumbled "Ok" I was always too embarrassed to tell anyone what he had done to punish me. I remained frightened of him forever.

Of course, when the boys came the following Wednesday I had to do exactly what I was supposed to do the first time. I took took off my clothes and showed them how they could please me. The following week the situation was reversed the boys took their clothes off and I had to show each one of them how a woman could please them. Of course, all the boys were over16 years old so there were no sexual laws being broken. The week after that I had to physically show them how to have sex in the missionary position, the following week it was a different position and then the next week a different position again and so it went on week after week. It continued for between two and three months. Then one Wednesday morning just as he was about to go out he shouted, "The boys won't be coming around tonight." For a split second, it was as if a very dark cloud had been lifted from over my head and I could almost start to smile again. Unfortunately, he followed it up with a statement that will burn itself through my heart forever. The statement was, "The older guys from the bar will be coming around for a refresher course, there will be about seven or eight of them." The front door slammed shut and he was gone.

I sank to my knees screaming and crying knowing that they were just going to use me for a "Gang Bang". I knelt there for about an hour, I had given up any thoughts of going to work, in fact at the end of that hour I had decided that I had taken as much as I could stand and my only option was suicide. Without any hesitation, I grabbed my handbag and walked out of the front door for the last time. I spent the whole morning going around various pharmacies and supermarkets purchasing as many painkiller tablets that I was allowed to. I finished off by purchasing two large bottles of my favourite brandy. I headed straight into a quiet wooded area at the rear of the houses where we lived. I came across a small hollow that was surrounded by thick bushes. I gave a quick glance around the area to make sure that nobody could see me. I squeezed through a bush, lay down on the grass and smiled. I continued to swallow painkillers whilst drinking Brandy from the bottle until suddenly I was sitting in the waiting room to enter phase two. As I mentioned earlier they allowed me into phase two because of my extreme circumstances. I was also assured that because of what he had done, Andy would never be allowed into phase two. So here I am with you and you have made my phase two life long fantasy come true and I am really very happy. We hugged and got dressed followed by a long passionate kiss then we parted company, both of us knowing that we would surely meet again.

Chapter 16
Some Bad News for Stuart

Stuart lay in his bed thinking about his latest experience with Nicky since arriving in phase two. He lay there with his hands clasped together at the back of his head. He started to put his experiences together, there was Sonia, there was Nicky and then he suddenly thought about the fantastic and very enjoyable time he had experienced with two girls that back in phase one, on earth, he hadn't even given a second thought to in a serious sexual way. It was then that he started to think to himself, "Wow" you really wouldn't want to miss out on getting into phase two if there was any way that you could know about it before it happened. How many other young ladies from his early teenage years might he yet get to meet and have more experiences that he didn't anticipate? He started to drop off to sleep, but of course as he was closing his eyes and drifting, he was thinking, "I can't wait to wake up and see what the next experience might be."

Stuart woke up totally refreshed, he jumped out of bed, showered and dressed quite quickly, and then he checked himself over in the mirror. He had a big smile across his face as he thought, "Yeah, I'm feeling pretty good." He turned around, walked across his room, opened the door and left feeling very confident. He ambled along at a slow pace taking in huge gulps of air through his nostrils and exhaling out of his mouth. A voice suddenly broke the silence, "Stuart my darling boy, how are you today?" Stuart looked behind him and to the right. As he did his face burst into an expression of sheer delight with the biggest smile ever. He turned, opened his arms as wide as he could and exclaimed, "Mother how absolutely wonderful to see you." His mother reciprocated and they hugged each other in a way that only a mother and son could ever experience.

Although Stuart hadn't been in phase two for very long, in that relatively short amount of time his demeanour was already reverting to the fun loving, good time, tough teenager that he used to be way back in phase one. As his head rested on his mother's shoulder and they hugged, a single tear of emotion trickled down his cheek.

After a minute or so they both stepped back from each other, Stuart quickly brushing the tear from his cheek before his mother had chance to see it. She hooked her arm into Stuart's and in a very relaxed manner they walked to a bench just ahead and sat down. As they sat down his mother was the first to speak, "Well my darling boy you must be finding phase two very amicable because you look so well." Stuart gave a big smile and replied, "Thanks Mum, you are absolutely right, I have met so many people from way back and quite honestly I've had the most fantastic time even though I haven't been here very long. There must be so many more people that I should be excited about seeing in the future. I haven't even had the opportunity to meet up with Dad yet and of course that's going to be a pretty nostalgic time as well." He waited for his Mum to reply, she didn't, she kept her head bowed down looking at her hands resting on her lap. After a while she slowly raised her head and looked at Stuart, he could see quite clearly that she was crying, silently. Then still visibly crying she spoke softly, "I'm afraid my son I've got some bad news for you." His mum burst into tears again, but now it was audible. Stuart put his arm around her again, hugged her, and spoke quietly into her ear. "Mum take your time and tell me all about it." She took hold of his hands and squeezed them, "Ok my darling I will." She began "After I had arrived here I had the opportunity to meet your Dad very early on. As you obviously know your Dad arrived in phase two three years before myself. I met him a couple of times just after I arrived. Then for some reason unknown to me at that time I didn't meet him for a long, long while. I thought it was very strange because on the couple of occasions when we had met it was super just like being on honeymoon all over again. I became very concerned about not seeing him and decided to go to the "Room for Unanswered Questions" to try and find out what had happened to him. I did find out what had happened to him and really it is so stupid. But first I have to tell you something about your Dad and how it used to be when we were in phase one. The way it was did pose a bit of a problem for me at times. The trouble was Stuart, your Dad was insanely jealous over me from the first day we started going out together. I will give you an example, after we had been together for about three years we got engaged to be married. We decided that we wouldn't go out so often, that would enable us to save and buy our own house when we did eventually get married. On one particular Saturday evening we bought a bottle of our favorite wine after making the decision to stop in and watch T.V., something that would normally bore the pants off both of us. On this particular Saturday there just happened to be a program that I was absolutely glued to. It was a program showing the most idolized pop stars from the 1960's, 70's and 80's. About half way through the program they had a piece on a pop singer that I used to be totally besotted with, as were millions of other women at the time. They suddenly showed a clip of him singing one of his biggest hits. His name was David Cassidy and the song he was singing was 'Daydreamer'. I was sitting on the couch and your Dad was sitting next to me with his arm around my shoulder just as if we were in the Cinema. David Cassidy had got about half way through his song when I just couldn't help myself, I burst into tears and screamed, "Oh David I love you." Your Dad was so jealous at what I had screamed that he stood up, walked across the room and he opened the Patio window as far as he could. He then bounced back across the room, put both of his arms around the T. V., he snatched it up, pulling the plug and all the connections out and marched into the garden. He walked down to the bottom of the garden, threw the T. V. onto the rubbish heap, picked up a huge log nearby and threw it straight through the screen. He turned around walked back up the garden and into the house through the patio window. He looked me directly in the eyes and said, "You can't love that it's just a bloody television, but you can love me because I'm real and I will always love you far more than a smashed-up television." That's how jealous your Dad was. Now I will tell you the reason for you not being able to see your Dad in phase two."

"When I explained in the "Office For Unanswered Questions" that since arriving in phase two I had met up with my husband, from phase one, on two occasions and that we had both had a wonderful time on each occasion. It seems that both of those occasions were a very long time ago and I couldn't understand why I never seemed to meet him although I found that I met up with people I had known in phase one who played a far less important role in my life on far more occasions."

"The lady I was talking to in the office was Valerie, she used to be my Gym teacher at school. She cleared up my misunderstanding, "Well Rita" she said, Rita was my mother's name, "Your husband suffered with what is considered a major problem here in phase two. I'm sure that you were always aware that your husband was insanely jealous with regards to you and I'm afraid it proved to be his downfall here in phase two. Shortly after your second meeting with him he met up with an old drinking pal from the days when you were courting. Now you will remember him telling you that his best mate, Alf, really fancied you. During their conversation, your husband started to accuse

Alf of having sex with you here in phase two. Eventually he completely and utterly convinced himself that his suspicions were true. The outcome was, your husband severely beat Alf up there and then on the spot. Something of course that just cannot be tolerated here in phase two. I'm afraid Rita your husband has been eliminated from phase two and will never be allowed here again." That my darling Stuart is, I'm afraid, the bad news. If it's in any way my fault that you won't see your Dad again I am desperately sorry." Stuart put his arms around his mum again, gave her another big hug and said, "mum it's definitely not your fault and I will always be here for you."

His mum looked up to him and said, "Thank you my darling son, now you tell me how you are settling down in phase two." "Well actually mum" he replied, "Apart from hearing the bad news that you have just given me I've really enjoyed my time here and of course everyone I've met has been so nice to me." His mother smiled at him and said, "I'm sure you've enjoyed it Stuart because you have probably realized by now, or at least started to realize, that life here in phase two is basically experiencing life as a permanent teenager." Stuart went quiet for a few seconds, then he looked his mum in the eye and said, "Do you know mum I think you may well be right."

"My darling son, you continue to enjoy your new found teenage years, but make sure you don't step out of line and make doubly sure that we meet again." Stuart gave his mum a huge hug and said, "I will mum, I have to go now but you have my word that you will definitely see me again. I love you far too much to risk not being able to see you again." They parted company and walked in opposite directions, there were tears welling very silently in both of their eyes.

Chapter 17
What Could Possibly Happen Next

When Stuart was back in his room and indulging in his favourite and only pastime, which was lying on his bed and summing up the days happening, he found that his thoughts were directly connected to his Mother. He suddenly realized that whenever he went through his door into the 'Hall' anything, absolutely anything at all, could happen. He drifted gently into his sleep whilst thinking, "I wonder what will happen when I wake up." After his body had recharged he showered, got dressed and ate his breakfast. Stuart walked to his door, put his hand on the handle and then before opening the door said to himself, "Ok here we go again and we will see what happens this time."

As Stuart strolled along without a care he began to chuckle very quietly to himself. He couldn't help thinking that he had no idea what might happen next. He then started to think, "I might meet my mum again or even my sister or perhaps an Aunty." It might be that the person he would next meet may not be a female but perhaps a buddy from his sporting days or even a guy he used to work with. Of course, if you were to be guided by recent events you are more likely to think his next meeting will be with someone of the opposite sex. It might be a young lady that he had made a friendly acquaintance with from the local take away or perhaps a friendly young lady who worked on the till in the supermarket. In fact, the possibilities of whoever he might meet next were limitless.

Interestingly what was to happen next was a little bit different to any happening that he had experienced up until now. Right up until this very moment in time, whenever Stuart had met someone in the hall that he used to know, he would just happen to be strolling along when a voice would call out his name from behind him and when he turned around he would see who it was.

On this occasion, it was very different. As Stuart strolled along he could see someone on his left-hand side and a short distance in front of him. He wasn't near enough to make out from the features who it really was. What he was one hundred per cent certain about was that he had seen the gate of the young ladies walk many times. As she got closer he recognized the tell-tale way her hair would flick from one side and then the other.

"Oh well" he thought, "The only way I'm going to find out is to give her a shout." He did exactly that, "Hi there how are you?" The young lady slowed right down and turned her head to face Stuart. A huge smile spread across Stuart's face, at the same time a huge smile spread across the young lady's face. Stuart was the first to speak, "Hi sweetheart how fantastic to see you." He held his arms wide open and immediately started to run towards her. As he did she immediately threw her arms open as wide as she could and started to run towards him. There arms enfolded each other in a passionate loving hug, as they did she screamed loudly, "My darling Stuart" at virtually the same moment Stuart shouted, "Sonia sweetheart."

Both of their tongues sought each other out frantically as they kissed for about five minutes. When they eventually stopped to take in air, they both took a step backwards to examine each other. Still holding both of each other's hands in front of themselves and with their arms outstretched Stuart was the first to speak again. "Wow Sonia you look absolutely sensational." Although she did look sensational she was dressed quite modestly. Her top was a bright green tee-shirt made from a nylon material that clung to her body in a quite provocative fashion. Because

Sonia was comparatively young she didn't wear a bra, although her breasts were large, very firm and of course a beautiful shape with hard tempting nipples pressing through the nylon material. She wasn't wearing the usual stretch pants, jeans or trousers either, instead she was wearing a type of Ra- Ra skirt, except that it was a little bit longer, just reaching her knees. It was a patterned skirt of orange and green, it matched the tee-shirt perfectly.

He said it a second time, "Wow Sonia you really do look sensational." He followed it up by saying something that completely took Sonia by surprise, "Sonia what do you think the chances are of us falling in love permanently?" Sonia paused for a while and then slowly replied, "Stuart darling, I think we need to go to your room, I'm afraid there are some serious issues that I need to talk to you about."

Stuart led the way without saying anything, he opened the door to his room and in they went. The first decision made was what each of them would have to drink. They both settled for a glass of red wine. Stuart happened to have a bottle of red wine that he knew Sonia particularly liked, he poured them both a glass as they sat alongside each other on the edge of the bed. It was then that Sonia started to mention the serious issues that she had previously mentioned to him. Stuart sat and listened. "My darling you have been here in phase two for a little while now and I know that you are beginning to appreciate some of the advantages here that were not an available option in phase one. But I'm afraid there are a few issues that you are not fully understanding clearly enough. First of all, my darling you are under the slight misapprehension that life here in phase two is some sort of extension to the life you had in phase one. I should tell you Stuart, that is a completely incorrect assumption, you have to understand that you have experienced a life on Earth for 62 years but you have, without any question, passed on from that life. Earth is now completely gone. The only connection you now have with that life on Earth is that all the people you meet here in your new life will be people you had an amicable relationship with on Earth. I do now, at this moment, have to explain to you that life on Earth is just a test to find out which people are good enough to be allowed into phase two. For example, you cannot intentionally cause the spillage of another human being's blood, it is also not acceptable to commit suicide or behave in a confrontational manner. When you have experienced phase two for quite some time you realize that when you were a little child on Earth, and grown-ups used to tell you that you only went to heaven if you were good was a statement a lot closer to the truth than anyone realized."

"What you also eventually understand is that there is no sickness, illness or violence in phase two and that no one brings any disability or sickness that they suffered from in phase one into phase two. You will also realize that because whatever happens between two people in phase two, stays with that couple on the occasions they meet, you can, therefore, fall in love with as many people as you wish knowing that it will always be a deep, honest and meaningful love that only the two-people involved will ever know about. Of course, however, the way this love between two people manifests itself is entirely up to them, no one else is ever going to know about it. Two people, therefore, are able to live out their wildest fantasies with as many individuals as they wish to and no one will ever know. So, my darling Stuart, the answer to your question is yes, I think that there is a wonderful chance of us falling very much in love. If you would like to know how I came to know the answers to all these questions I can tell you that I went to the "Room of Unanswered Questions" and asked them. I hope I've saved you the trouble of doing the same thing."

"Now my darling Stuart let's get back to dealing with the situation that has been presented to us. If I remember correctly during our last meeting I believe I took control and we more or less did everything that I suggested and although I think we both thoroughly enjoyed ourselves we didn't actually fuck. When we parted company, I promised you that at our next meeting you could be completely in charge and we will do whatever you choose". Sonia stood about one meter in front of Stuart, looked into his eyes and said, "I am now at your wish and command my darling."

Stuart had sat there all that time without uttering a sound but now suddenly found himself sitting there with a sensational looking young lady standing in front of him waiting to obey his instructions. Once again, for a minute or so, he was shocked. After the minute or so had passed he let that big smile, the one that usually melted most women's feelings, spread across his face. He leaned back slightly with his hands stretched out behind him and rested on the bed, and then broke the silence "Sonia, my sweetheart, you are an absolute gem." Then without hesitating he said, "Could you bring that chair over here for me?" He pointed to a hard-backed chair standing in the corner, it was the type of chair that you would normally sit on to perhaps eat a meal at a table.

Sonia didn't make any comment. She turned around, walked across the room, picked up the chair and placed it just in front of Stuart. Stuart immediately said, "Ok sweetheart you sit there, face me with that lovely smile and take your top off for me." Sonia did exactly as he requested, as she lifted the top over her breasts, although they were young and firm, they still bobbed up and down a little, of course her nipples were as usual already quite hard. Stuart could already feel an erection stirring between his legs, but that was nothing unusual either. Sonia threw her top on the floor and said, "Ok darling what's next?" Without hesitating Stuart said, "What I would like you to do is lean forward and put your tongue into my mouth as far as you can and keep it as still and as straight as you possibly can." Stuart opened his mouth and Sonia did as he asked, Stuart then closed his lips on Sonia's tongue as hard as he could just as if he were trying to suck a lollipop off its stick. When he needed to he would take a huge breath of air and he would suck as hard as he could again, every time he sucked on her tongue he could hear her moan. After about a minute he stopped and took his lips away from her tongue. Sonia gave a little gasp, put her hands around the back of Stuarts neck and said, "Wow Stuart that was really turning me on, I could feel a sensation between my legs every time you sucked hard."

Stuart gave her his big smile again and replied, "Well that's great sweetheart so how would you like to stand up on that chair and face me?" Sonia didn't hesitate she stood up and stepped onto the chair. Stuart instantly slid his hand up between her legs until it came to a stop "Oh yes" he said, "You must have been really turned on because I can feel that it is very damp up there, now you really don't want to be wearing damp panties do you?" He didn't wait for a reply, he slid both hands under her skirt and took hold of the elastic around the top of her panties and pulled them down. He asked her to lift one foot at a time, removed her panties and dropped them onto the floor. He leaned back and said, "There you are sweetheart that must feel a lot better?" Sonia gave Stuart a big smile and said, "Yes my darling I'm quite happy about everything so far."

Stuart turned his head upwards to look between Sonia's cleavage and into her eyes, at the same time he said, "Sweetheart will you hold your skirt up high enough for me to see everything?" "Of course I will my darling," she replied. She grasped the hem of her skirt and lifted it up to her waist where she held it so that Stuart could see everything. Stuart's erection was growing with every move, directly in front of his eyes now was Sonia's bush of hair. He put his arms around her and cupped the cheeks of her bottom in his hands, he didn't apply any pressure but Sonia moved her abdomen forward so that her bush pressed into Stuart's face. He didn't move for a minute he just took in her womanly smell. Stuart leaned back and said, "Sweetheart will you take that skirt off now and let me have a look at you?" Sonia didn't say anything she undid the button and the zipper on her skirt, let it fall around her ankles and then kicked it across the floor. Stuart was still leaning back and without hesitation, with his eyes fixed upon her he said, "Sonia you are now completely naked and you are exquisite." He followed that statement by saying as he stood up, "Sonia I'm pretty warm myself now." He stood up and removed all his clothes, then with one arm around her back and the other one curled underneath her knees he scooped her off the chair and stood her on the floor in front of the chair. He immediately sat down on the chair and looking slightly upwards into Sonia's eyes he said, "Sweetheart I want you to fuck me." Once again Sonia didn't say anything, she took a step forward so that she had one leg either side of Stuart's legs. She looked down to see Stuart's erection just below her vagina. As she leaned forward and closed her arms around Stuart's neck she lowered herself. Stuart's erection was so hard and Sonia was so wet that he entered her without any directional help from either of them. Sonia continued to rise up and then glide down on him for what seemed forever at the same time licking and nibbling his ear. Sonia reached a climax first, as soon as the groan of pleasure had finished coming from her mouth she immediately stood up and kneeled between his legs, she lowered her head and continued pleasing him until his groan of pleasure could be heard coming from his mouth. They both stood up, engulfed each other in their arms and then flopped sideways onto the bed. There was no movement and no sound, they were both spent so much that they drifted into a warm and comforting sleep whilst locked in each other's arms.

Chapter 18
Analyzing the Situation

Both Stuart and Sonia awoke pretty much together, they did at last, both express to each other that they loved each other deeply. They both knew that those feelings would never change. Now that they were in phase two they also knew that nothing would change the way their relationship manifested itself other than when they parted company, and even then, the both of them had said they were sure that they would be meeting again. During their final hug and kiss goodbye at the end of their meeting Stuart whispered into Sonia's ear, "At or next meeting sweetheart we do everything that you want to do."

After that meeting with Sonia, Stuart took to his bed to have a good rest in preparation for what his next meeting might entail There was a slight change in his habits following his last meeting with Sonia, considering the good talking to that she had given him. One of the changes in habit was that at the end of each day he would, whilst lying in bed, analyze everything that had happened to him during the previous day. He lay there with his hands behind his head on the pillow. Obviously, what his thoughts were deeply involved in was the meeting he had just spent with Sonia. The first thing he began analyzing was everything that she had explained to him whilst giving him what could only be described as a jolly good lecture. After he'd finished thinking over everything that she had brought to his attention, he turned his thoughts to the wonderful, glorious, fantastic sex that he had enjoyed right through to a very satisfying climax.

It was then, after recalling all the events that had taken place, he wondered whether there was any information that he could glean from those events that could possibly enhance future events. The practice of analyzing everything at the end of any day was something that his mother suggested that he should always do. After going over his latest meeting with Sonia and taking into account the previous events that had taken place since he had arrived in phase two he had now come to a few conclusions.

First of all, there is no doubt that life in phase two is, without question, of a far higher quality than it is in phase one. Although there are occasions in phase two when you hear about rare events such as the one that involved his dad that do take place. Generally speaking time is mostly taken up with genuine physical love such as his experiences with Sonia and Nicky, but also genuine psychological love as experienced when meeting his mother.

It was now logical to think that in the future, knowing that there were many other women he could recall from phase one, there was a real possibility of there being many more different experiences and of course many more women of a similar age to Sonia and Nicky. Of course, there was also a possibility of others that would appear as old as they were when Stuart had known them in phase one, that meant they could appear considerably older than himself.

Stuart hadn't forgotten there was also very many male friends in phase one and although at this moment in time he had to consider what benefit, if any, could be gained by having a second meeting with a male friend in phase two. The main reason that he could think of for there not being a good reason for meeting old male friends was because the main talking point of male friends on Earth was basically, "How did you get on with your date last night," but of course that particular line of conversation would not be acceptable or normal in phase two.

Summing up, from the conclusions Stuart had thought long and hard about he decided that because, up to this moment in time, he had found life in phase two interesting, exciting and very enjoyable it was probably best to take each event that comes along in his stride and to continue enjoying them in just the same way that he already had been doing. But of course, there was one other thought that was very much on his mind and that was, would the time ever come when he would become fed up or bored at settling down in his bed after his latest event, and wondering what was going to happen the next time he went for a stroll out into the Hall of Second Greetings. He wasn't too long dwelling on this thought before he had a suspicion that there might be a way of finding out what would happen if he became so bored that he decided he wouldn't even bother to go out of his door.

The decision he had come to was that he could go to the Office for Unanswered Questions and enquire if it was at all possible to move on in phase two so that he wouldn't be just waiting for surprise events to happen and hopefully seek a situation that was possibly more constructive. After a little while, considering this thought, he decided that as he was enjoying his second existence in phase two so he was quite happy to continue as things were. However, the Office for Unanswered Questions was definitely a reasonable option for the future. He let his eyes gently close and he drifted into a deep and satisfying sleep.

Chapter 19
A Holiday Memory

When Stuart had woken up from his sleep all the thoughts of his previous analysis of the situation quickly flooded back through his mind. Without hesitation, he happily got out of his bed and prepared himself for the next adventure. At this moment in time the nature of the next event was completely unknown to him. He showered, had a good breakfast and dressed to go out. He now found himself dressing like he used to when he was in his late teens and early twenties, just as he used to before he met Nathalie. That was the time when he would go out hoping to have one of the good times that nearly always used to happen during those years. Another phenomenon that occurred in phase two was that whenever he went to his wardrobe to get dressed, there was always exactly the clothes that he wanted to wear hanging there.

This particular day he had decided to wear a pair of black jeans and a yellow nylon stretch polo neck top, which of course showed off his very enviable physique to its best. He tidied his hair and stepped out into The Hall of Second Greetings. He ambled along with his hands in his pockets obviously hoping that something would happen. Of course, when anyone strolled out into the Hall they had to hope something would happen because all there ever was to look at as you strolled through were the Marble benches that were scattered about, should you wish to sit down, and a few rather attractive flower boxes that were dotted about. As on all the previous occasions Stuart had ventured out to stroll it wasn't long before he heard a voice break the silence. The only difference this time was that Stuart could not believe what he was hearing. What he could hear was a young ladies voice calling out, "Hi there Stuart how are you?" The voice was in a broken English accent with definitely a Spanish flavor. Immediately, without turning around he knew it was the voice of Wanetta. He spun around, held his arms out as wide as he possibly could and ran towards her. At the same time, she threw her arms out as wide as she could and ran towards him. As they ran towards each other Stuart was shouting, "Wanetta" and Wanetta was screaming out, "Stuart". As they closed together they embraced each other in a way that could only be described as full of joy. They both kissed each other on the cheek three times and then embraced again. The most surprising element about the whole meeting was that they had never had any physical contact with each other before this meeting.

How did they know each other? Well, they had actually only been in the company of each other on one occasion for about five or six hours. That was when Stuart was 21 and he had gone on holiday to the Dominican Republic with three of his friends from the football club. His meeting with Wanetta happened when he and his three friends were in a night club on the last night of their holiday and they were sharing an eight seat semi-circular cubical with Wanetta and her two friends. Unfortunately, because there were four guys and only three girls it made splitting up together a bit awkward. The guys weren't prepared to leave one of themselves without a partner and one of the girls was prepared to make up a threesome. The outcome was that at the end of the evening although they had all enjoyed a fantastic time together it ended with them wishing each other the very best wishes for the future and parting, probably thinking that they would never meet again. That thought was absolutely wrong because here they were, Stuart and Wanetta, locked in a very warm embrace. The fact that Stuart and Wanetta had met up again is probably not too surprising because on that night in the Dominican Republic the magnetism between the two of them was very strong. The initial reason Stuart was drawn to Wanetta so strongly was that, although she had a very pleasant personality, during the conversation they held together he discovered that she was from Miami and even more interestingly her full-time self-employment was to attend many varieties of functions and events as a Beyoncé look alike, who was one of the top three pop singers at that time. It had to be said that she did, and still does, bare a remarkable resemblance to Beyoncé from head to foot.

They released their embrace, stepped back from one another and gazed at each other with a huge beaming smile on both of their faces. Wanetta was first to speak, "Oh Stuart I am so pleased you returned my call because I was really frightened that you wouldn't speak to me after I left you in the Dominican Republic and I never even kissed you goodbye." Stuart was now starting to really understand how life worked in phase two and he was determined not to let this opportunity take a minute longer than it needed to. Stuart replied, "As soon as I turned around and saw that it was you Wanetta my first thought was, I think that gorgeous looking Spanish, Miami girl owes me a kiss, so Wanetta I will have that kiss now if that's ok with you?" There was no answer from Wanetta, she stepped forward, put both of her hands around the back of Stuart's head, and pulled him towards her. At first, she licked Stuart all over his face, she then opened her mouth wide and kissed him veraciously, at the same time pressing her cunt against Stuart's penis.

Once again Stuart didn't waste any time responding. He put both of his arms around her and grabbed the cheeks of her bottom firmly. At the same time he pulled her even harder against his penis. Right on cue, as usual, Stuart felt his penis immediately spring into an erection. Wanetta also immediately felt his erection press against her slit. She automatically reached down with her right hand, unzipped his jeans and put her hand inside. She grabbed hold of his cock and started to rhythmically rub it up and down. Both of their tongues were now feeding frantically on the wetness of each other's mouth.

Suddenly Wanetta stopped rubbing Stuart's penis, she took her hand out of his pants, stopped kissing him and stepped back. Stuart was a little bit taken aback. Then she looked up at him and said, "Stuart we have to stop now, it's really much too soon for you to come, we have a lot more to do. I think it's best if we go back to my room as quickly as possible."

Chapter 20
Back at Wanetta's

They had both run all the way. Wanetta entered her room first, and Stuart followed. When he was inside he leaned back on the door and it clicked shut. Stuart had run all the way back about two paces behind Wanetta, she was wearing a pair of very tight and very brief, green shorts with an orange opened neck shirt at the top. All the way back he couldn't help staring at the cheeks of her bottom as they went rhythmically from side to side. He couldn't help thinking that about five minutes ago he was squeezing both of those cheeks in his hands and of course now that they were inside the closed room he was eager to continue from where he had left off. He immediately walked towards her, as she turned around he was ready to put both of his hands on her waist just above the hips. To Stuart's absolute amazement Wanetta stepped back and said, "No Stuart, you have to wait." Stuart dropped his hands and said, "Ok babe, is there a problem?" Wanetta put her hands on her hips, smiled and said to him, "Stuart you are a naughty boy, you have to wait until I dance for you. When I have finished dancing for you I will know then that you will be ready to fuck me properly, ok?" It was one of the very rare occasions that caused Stuart to stutter, "Yeah sure Wanetta whatever you say, so where do you want me to be at this moment?"

"That's very good Stuart, now we can begin to have a good time. Grab that chair over there and put it here in the middle of the room, then you must sit down on it." He wasted no time in doing as she asked. Just as he sat down on the chair Wanetta switched her music on and of course it was just as you would have expected, fast, rhythmic, Latin American music. As Wanetta began making her way back towards Stuart her body started to move with the music.

Slowly to start with but the nearer she got to Stuart the faster her rhythm and movements became. First it was her shoulders, then her boobs, followed by her hips and then finally, expressing it in Miami language, her booty. When she reached him, whilst continuing to gyrate to the music, and without stopping gyrating she moved around behind him. Suddenly her arm stretched over his shoulder and into the front of his face she was dangling her shirt, after a few seconds she threw the shirt across the room. It then became perfectly obvious to him that she wasn't wearing a bra. The reason he knew that was because he could feel her shaking her naked breast against his right cheek then his left cheek and then his right cheek again. Stuart turned his head slightly to both sides in turn. He was well aware that she had the most gorgeous coffee coloured skin. Now he could quite clearly see the very dark and very large aureoles with very large, dark and hard nipples adorning her beautiful breasts. All this time the Latin music was driving her to continue what was now becoming a very sensual dance. She danced around to the front of him but kept her back facing him. Suddenly she spun around, faced him, and started to rhythmically shimmer closer to him. When she was close enough she started to shake the top half of her body from side to side which enabled her to keep gently smacking each side of his face with her tits. Each time her breast stroked his cheek Stuart would quickly turn his head to the side and try to lick each nipple as it passed by his mouth.

Wanetta suddenly shimmered a couple of paces backwards. She lifted both hands and with the index finger of each hand pointed downwards towards the front of the little green shorts which of course was now the last thing that she was wearing. Wanetta never wore panties. The only conclusion to be made from this gesture was that she wanted him to take her shorts off. He leaned forward and undid the press stud. As he did he looked up into her face, she had a big smile and at the same time was giving him a nod of approval. He continued, carefully undoing the zipper on the front of her shorts, they immediately dropped down around her ankles, she stepped out of them and kicked them across the room.

She continued dancing to the music, Stuart could see quite clearly that she didn't have a 'Hollywood' or a 'Brazilian', but a very neat triangle of dark curly hair. Wanetta had been dancing for quite some time and naturally she was now starting to perspire. He could see the perspiration on her beautiful coffee colored skin, it was trickling down her neck, through her cleavage and then all the way down until it disappeared into the bush of curly dark hair between her thighs.

Wanetta noticed that Stuart was showing signs of frustration. She could see that periodically his hand, probably without him realizing it, would press his erection in a downward movement and of course the animal lust inside him was building up quite considerably. She beckoned him up to stand and take his shirt off, he didn't hesitate, his shirt was off and across the room before he had even finished standing up. Wanetta immediately took one step forward and grabbed hold of his cock. She looked up into his eyes and gave a big smile, at the same time she said, "Stuart you know you are very big across your shoulders but down around your tummy you are quite small and then you get big down here again." She squeezed his cock really hard and said "I think that by squeezing you there Stuart my dancing has been good because I think you are ready to fuck me really good." She undid his belt and zipper then pushed his trousers and pants down to his ankles. Stuart stepped out of them and kicked them across the floor. Then with one arm around her lower body, his hand clutching her bottom, and his other arm around her upper body with his hand at the back of her head, he scooped her clean off her feet and pulled her towards him. Wanetta instinctively wrapped her legs around his waist and locked her ankles together behind his back. Stuart brought his right hand back underneath her, he grabbed hold of his cock and guided it into her vagina just as he thrust forward.

Although Wanetta was sexually very excited, turned on and very wet, as Stuart thrust forward there was still a tight feeling as he entered her. In fact, it was definitely tight enough to make Wanetta give out a squeal of pleasure on each following thrust. Stuart didn't just thrust into her but as he did he kept lifting her up and down in a rocking motion with both of his hands clutching the cheeks of her bottom. It didn't take long, Wanetta suddenly during their frenzied, lustful fucking shouted out, "Stuart I'm coming, Stuart I'm coming!" He felt her body go limp, he spun around so that the bed was behind Wanetta. He lifted her off himself and dropped her onto the bed. She lay there spread eagled as she looked up at him. Without a second's hesitation, he grabbed her by the ankles and dragged her towards the edge of the bed. He put her legs up against his chest and let her heels rest on his shoulders. He then grabbed his cock and entered her again. Then whilst holding one ankle in each hand he began thrusting rhythmically into her again and again. Although Wanetta had already reached her climax she still groaned with pleasure on every thrust. Once again it wasn't long before Stuart gave out the male groan of pleasure upon reaching his climax. Without withdrawing from her, he lifted her up, turned around and let himself, with Wanetta still clinging to him, fall back on the bed. Within seconds they both drifted into a comfortable sleep whilst still in that position.

Chapter 21
Such Diverse Reasons

Wanetta woke first to find herself stretched out on top of Stuart with her head resting comfortably on his chest. Without moving she let her eyes glance upwards to see that he was still fast asleep. She gently leaned up with one arm either side of his chest. Wanetta's erotic idea of waking him up was to dangle one nipple onto his lips and then the other one, she continued alternatively until Stuart's eyes opened. His alert mind knew instantly what the situation was and exactly what she was doing. He responded without moving and parted his lips every time she lowered her nipples and let them enter his mouth, he would then give each one a firm squeeze with his lips. There was about five seconds gone when Wanetta could feel his erection pressing up between her legs. She immediately sat up on his midriff, lowered her hand and guided his cock inside her. This time she did all the work and fucked him hard whilst in the sitting position. About four minutes later they had both climaxed again and were lying back resting. Stuart had his arm around Wanetta and she was curled up beside him with her head on his shoulder.

Stuart looked down into her eyes and spoke, "Wanetta we've been together for some hours and I think it's time we engaged in a normal conversation for a while." A big smile spread across her face as she replied, "Ok Stuart if we must." Even then she stretched down and squeezed his cock, oh floppy, floppy," she giggled. Stuart spoke again, "Ok babe let's start by you telling me how you came to be here in phase two." Stuart was now beginning to find it quite interesting to listen to the different stories people had to tell about who chose their destiny and what the options were that they had to choose from. Wanetta gazed upwards as she began her story. "Well Stuart it was my aunty Lily who got to choose my destiny. Now I do know what the two options were but the jury is still out with regards to me being happy with the choice that Aunty Lily made. The first option was that when I became sixty years old I would start suffering with rheumatoid arthritis, never the less I would live on until I reached seventy-seven years old at which stage I would catch a really bad bout of pneumonia and pass on from phase one. I can tell you Stuart that Aunty Lily didn't choose that option." "Ok babe tell me what option she did choose for you that you think maybe wasn't the best choice." "Well" she replied, still gazing into the air, "I was fifty-six years old, still healthy, fit and very attractive so I am told. I wasn't married and at that age I didn't really have any reason to stay at home for long periods of time. I'd made plenty of money as a look-alike so I spent most of my time travelling around the world seeing different places. On this particular occasion, my very good friend Alesha and I had decided to take a coach tour through the Andes in Peru. My Aunt Lily chose that there would be a terrible avalanche and our coach would be pushed over a cliff and into a deep ravine with no survivors. Now the problem I have is that when they eventually recover the bodies I have no way of knowing whether I looked respectable, because Stuart, although I spent many years doing very sexy dancing like Beyoncé, I was always respectable. I would like to add Stuart that although being pushed over a cliff in a coach sounds a pretty grim way to go its actually, one minute your sitting on a coach in phase one and the next thing you experience is waking up in a bed with someone you knew years ago coming up to you and explaining what has happened. So there is no grim experience at all and so long as you've been a good citizen during your time in phase one it's all pretty good." Stuart gave out a little bit of a chuckle and said, "Actually babe I think I completely agree with you. I'd love to hear about whose destiny you chose."

Wanetta looked at him and put her hand over her mouth as if she didn't want to answer the question. After what seemed to Stuart to be a very long time she broke the silence. "Ok Stuart if you'd really like to know who my choice was for I'll tell you. It just happened to be my young nephew. There was only a couple of years difference in age between my mother and her brother, but the reason I had a much younger nephew was because my mother had me when she was only twenty years old, but her Brother was almost forty-five when my nephew Sonny was born, I think I was about twenty-three years old then. When it came to me choosing Sonny's destiny it became very awkward because at the time I chose his destiny he was already thirty-one years old and when I tell you what the choices were I'm sure you will agree with me that it was a bit awkward."

"The first choice was that he would reach the age of seventy-two and then he would have a massive stroke from which he would never recover, he would pass on three days later. The second choice was that when he reached thirty-four years of age he would have an argument with a guy down at Miami Docks. The argument would turn into a brawl, Sonny would be stabbed and would die almost immediately from the wound. Wanetta went quiet and there was silence again. "Ok" Stuart said, "And" Wanetta suddenly almost started shouting at Stuart, "Well I have to tell you, although nobody has ever known before because I kept it a secret to myself, I absolutely hated Sonny. I know he was only a lad but he did things that I can never forgive him for and because of that I made the second choice that he would be stabbed when he was thirty-four years old and I have no regrets about making that choice. There was silence again, Stuart let the silence hang there for a couple of minutes before he leaned over, kissed her on the forehead and said, "Not to worry babe, why don't you tell me why you hated him so much?" "Ok" she said. Well the problem was that I never got married and I lived with my mother until I was about thirty eight years old. Because mum and her brother tried to make financial matters easier for both families we all lived together in one house. When I was about thirty-five years old and Sonny was about twelve, that was when the trouble started."

"At that time Sonny started to have a couple of friends around for sleepovers. The first thing that began to happen was that when I was showering Sonny would burst into the bathroom and shout, hey guys I'm in the bathroom, come and have a look at this quick. All three of them would then stand there staring at me through the clear glass cubicle. I complained to mum and told her that she would have to have words with my nephew about his behaviour. It obviously didn't do any good because not only did it not stop, their bad behaviour escalated quite considerably. The next thing that started happening was that the three of them would creep into my bedroom late into the night when everyone was asleep. I would wake up when the single white cotton sheet would be snatched off my bed, of course the nights were so hot in Miami that it was virtually compulsory to sleep naked, which of course I did. Everyone naturally wondered why I didn't shout out for help, but of course as soon as the sheet came off me and I woke up one of them would put his hand over my mouth and the other two would hold my arms and legs. They would then quickly grope me over the whole of my body and run out. It would always only last two or three minutes and they would be back in bed pretending to be fast asleep. If I ever complained about it to anyone the boys would always stick together and swear that I was making it all up. That's it then Stuart, now you know why I hated him, the sooner I could choose for him to get his just deserve the happier I was." Stuart squeezed Wanetta closer to him and said, "Thanks for sharing that with me babe, I think enough said about all that we will move on and continue to enjoy phase two." Wanetta put her arms around Stuart and hugged him back.

Suddenly Stuart jumped off the bed and held his hand out for Wanetta, at the same time he said, "We've had a really good session today but I think it's about time both of us got back to our own room." Wanetta gave him her big smile and replied, "I'm sure you're right Stuart but shall we fuck one more time?" Stuart gave a little laugh and said, "Babe do you think I could ever refuse a fuck with you?" Before he had time to finish off what he was going to say Wanetta interrupted him, "You'd better not Stuart because if you do I'll bite your balls off!" Stuart smiled and finished off what he was going to say, "I definitely wouldn't refuse a fuck babe, but would you mind if I asked for a rain check just at the moment?" Wanetta smiled and said, "Ok honey, give me a big wet kiss and I'm gone." Stuart did just that, he put his tongue as far into her as he could and he let the wetness of his lips completely cover her mouth. As soon as he had finished, without saying a word, Wanetta turned and started to walk away. She made one last gesture as she started to move away. She leaned back, gave his cock a really good squeeze. Stuart smiled and said, "Thanks babe."

Chapter 22
A Bit of Soul Searching.

As soon as Stuart had left Wanetta he headed back to his room. He made himself a coffee and then flopped back onto his bed with his hands clasped together at the back his head. He lay there recalling how well it had all gone, and of course as usual he had spent a very pleasant few hours with Wanetta, just as he had with the all the ladies he had made an acquaintance with in phase one and now in phase two. Of course, since meeting them in phase two again he had now met them on many occasions. It has to be said that every meeting had ended with the most pleasurable outcome as the first.

Obviously, there weren't just the ladies already mentioned involved, there were many other very nice ladies, young and older that Stuart was able to have a second meeting with. For instance, there was Gina who used to be the waitress at a very nice Italian Restaurant he used to go to. Then of course there was Yani, a very sexy masseuse at his local Chinese Massage Parlor, which naturally brings to mind immediately, Monica who was also a masseuse only at a Swedish Massage Parlor. There was even his Aunty Lizzie who just happened to be only ten or eleven years older than he was. It appears that when Stuart reached his teenage years Aunt Lizzie was quite smitten with him. The list doesn't end there, many more phase one acquaintants made themselves available to Stuart and as mentioned earlier they would all have a similar pleasurable outcome. As anyone could imagine Stuart's existence in phase two continued in this manner for quite a long period of time, things changed slightly after Stuart had spent another fantastic session with Sonia. He had arrived back to his room and as usual made a coffee and crashed onto his bed to lie back and mull over his latest event. Strangely on this occasion his thoughts followed a slightly different pattern.

What he was thinking of at that moment in time was that his existence in phase two had almost been a one hundred percent fantastic time of which he could make no complaints. Well who in their right mind could ever complain about an existence where the whole of your time was taken up by making love and having mind blowing sex every day with women that you had known and liked all through your first existence in phase one. As Stuart had told himself, there was nothing anyone could ever complain about, but he was starting to wonder if it was at all possible that there was something else in phase two that he could ever become involved with. The obvious next question he would ask himself was "Is there anything other than fucking in phase two and if so how could he possibly find out about it?

Of course, it didn't take long before the answer to that question came into his mind. Yes, I can go to the Office for Unanswered Questions and ask. It wasn't very long before he had come to a final decision on the matter, about what he would do to solve the problem. There was one final thought that he had to clear up. He had to try and remember to whom it was that he spoke to on his last visit to this particular office. Actually it was quite a simple problem to solve, he remembered almost immediately, it was his old headmaster Conrad Edwards. Stuart decided that as soon as he had taken his usual rest he would be going straight to the office. He lay on his bed and drifted into his sleep almost instantly. It wasn't very long before he was awake again feeling refreshed and having a strong urge to get himself ready and go for a stroll into the hall to see if he would have a meeting. He controlled the urge and said to himself, "No I'm going to the office as soon as I've had coffee."

Stuart walked towards the sign that said The Office for Unanswered Questions. As he got nearer he could see the outline of a door, he walked directly towards it. He got within two paces of the door when the same message as before in green lights suddenly lit up across the door. "Please State Your Name." Without hesitation Stuart answered the request, "Stuart Gifford." Barely a few seconds had passed when the lights on the door changed from green to red and the message then said, "You May Enter," and the door opened automatically. As Stuart stepped inside and looked around, the room was almost exactly as he had remembered it with just one slight difference, Conrad Edwards was, this time, seated in his chair facing Stuart as he approached the desk. As soon as Stuart was close enough to the desk Conrad stood up and held out a hand to greet Stuart. Just as Stuart took hold of his hand Conrad spoke, "Welcome Stuart, it is so nice to see you and even nicer to hear that you've become a big favourite out in the Hall." Stuart smiled and answered, "Thank you very much Conrad and I must say it is very nice to talk to you again." Conrad chuckled, "Thank you Stuart, but of course judging by what I've heard in phase two, I'm pretty sure you've come here with something for us to talk about and not just to see me." He chuckled again. "I certainly have Conrad. I've got a question that I'm hoping you can answer for me." "Ok Stuart fire away," he replied in a more serious tone. Stuart leaned forward, clasped his hands together and rested his forearms on the desk, he took in a big gulp of air and began.

"Well I've been here in phase two for quite some time now and I feel I've grasped the joy of life in phase two with both hands. Having done that I must say that there couldn't possibly be a better place or way of life anywhere to live a perpetual existence than being in phase two. I am hoping that now I've said that, nobody underestimates how much I love phase two. The problem is I'm inclined to get a little bit bored on occasions and I just wonder sometimes if it's possible to spend some time involved in something other than fucking. I am aware that my question may make some people think that I am ungrateful, I sincerely hope that it doesn't."

Stuart sat there and waited for Conrad's response. He was kept there sitting for quite a few minutes in silence. Conrad shuffled in his seat before looking Stuart directly in the eyes and in a very serious manner began his reply, "Alright Stuart, the first thing I wish to say is that I understand your sentiments entirely. The second point I would make is that you are definitely not the first person to come into the office with that question. Basically, you want to know if there is anything else you can occupy your time doing, am I correct Stuart?" "Absolutely Conrad." Conrad rested his arms on the desk and for about two minutes stared down at the desk without saying anything. Suddenly without any warning Conrad stood up and walked around the desk. As he approached Stuart he held out his hand, obviously for a handshake, at that moment Conrad spoke, "Stuart, I'd like you to leave your request with me and I will put it forward to the committee of decisions. I will let you know the outcome as soon as possible." Stuart thanked him very much and left the office. As he strolled back to his room he couldn't help wondering if anything would develop from his request.

Chapter 23
Just Passing the Time

Stuart was strolling back to his room probably at a slower pace than usual mainly because the thoughts that were totally dominating his mind were completely about what the reaction would be to him confessing he was bored some of the time. He was staring down at his feet as he took every step when suddenly he heard a shout loud enough to make him look up, he heard the voice again. "Stuart, my darling Stuart I'm over here." He spun around and there to his complete amazement was Nicky and she was looking absolutely stunning. Stuart held his arms open wide as they walked towards each other, when they were close enough Stuart let his arms envelope Nicky and squeeze her so hard that for a couple of seconds she was completely breathless. As he stepped back he gave her his usual big beaming smile and said, "High babe, how wonderful to meet up with you again, you look absolutely fantastic." "Thank you darling, it's really nice to hear you say that." They took each other in their arms and passionately French kissed for about five minutes. Stuart spoke first, "What's the plan now babe, any ideas?" Nicky gave a little bit of a giggle and replied, "Stuart I don't think that our plans have ever stretched any further than having a good sex session so if that's good for you we could head straight back to my room." Stuart grabbed hold of her hand and said, "That sounds good to me, lead the way."

Once they had stepped inside Nicky's room Stuart closed the door and walked over to the bed, sat down and proceeded to take his shoes off. Whilst he was doing that Nicky called over to him, "Want a coffee my darling?" "Sure thing" Stuart replied. Nicky set about making the coffee and Stuart continued to take the rest of his clothes off. When he was completely naked he lay on the bed and waited for Nicky. She walked over to the bed and put the two coffees on the small bedside table next to where Stuart was lying. She sat down on the edge of the bed next to him so that she was facing him but also sideways to his naked body. In quite a casual manner she took his cock in her hand and started to gently rub it up and down at the same time she looked at Stuart and spoke, "My darling Stuart we have a lot of great sex when we meet up and I want you to know that I love it." Stuart let his hand rest on her thigh and replied, "That's great babe because I've always loved the sex we have as well." Nicky sat there still gently rubbing his cock, she leaned forward and rested her head on his chest before saying, "The thing is my darling, I want to ask you a favour." Stuart stroked her hair and said, "No problem babe ask away." "Well" she said," "You are the only person to ever know that I committed suicide because I was being sexually abused and the only reason I was allowed into phase two was because of the extreme provocation. But the issue I want to ask you about with regards to the favour I mentioned is, prior to all the abuse happening, I remember quite well that when the girls got together and we had a night out at the pub for a good old chin-wag the night would usually end with us talking about our latest sexual exploits. I can't help remembering some of the girls who had steady partners and boyfriends for quite a lengthy period of time and were really in love with their respective partners saying that quite often their night would end with their men taking them from behind sometimes quite roughly and in a demanding way. The difference for them was that it was being done on a mutually and consenting basis between two people who loved each other. Consequently, the girls would say that they enjoyed the experience just as much as the men. So Stuart, my favour is this, I would love it if you would take me from behind, and if you do feel the urge to be rough or demanding with me I'm perfectly happy about that as well." Nicky stopped talking, she continued to lie there with her head resting on his chest and still gently rubbing his cock. She waited for a reply from Stuart. It didn't take him long to realize that she had finished asking her favour. Stuart spoke, "Babe if that's the favour you're asking how could I possibly refuse? We can start as soon as you are ready." Nicky tilted her head upwards, looked into Stuart's eyes and said, "Thank you my darling, I love you so much. She then lowered her head over Stuart's waist, she took his cock into her mouth and gave one long suck before jumping very quickly off the bed. She stood at the side of the bed next to where Stuart was lying and began removing her clothes.

Stuart lay back without saying anything. Nicky pulled her tee shirt up and over her head, she didn't need to wear a bra her breasts were large but very firm and pointed, he watched her titties bobble up and down. She undid her jeans and let them fall to the floor, she then slid her panties down, as she bent over to slide them off her feet Stuart suddenly swung out with his hand and slapped Nicky hard across the cheeks of her bottom. At the same time he shouted out, "What are you fucking about at girl, are you going to get your arse over here onto this bed? You can see quite clearly I've got a really good hard on so how long are you going to keep me waiting?" Nicky straitened up immediately, rushed around the bed and quickly lay down. As she was rushing around the bed she called out to Stuart, "I'm sorry darling I didn't mean to keep you waiting, I love you so much you can fuck me as long as you like, I love you Stuart, I love you."

She flopped onto the bed and lay back with her head on the pillow. Stuart glared at her for a minute and then with a rather threatening tone in his voice he said, "Are you fucking stupid girl? You know that when you've done something to displease me you don't get fucked lying on your back. You get up onto your hands and knees and tell me that you're ready." Nicky looked up at him and said very timidly, "Stuart what have I done to displease you?" "Are you fucking kidding me?" he replied. "Didn't you just suck my cock once and then stop without my permission, now get on all fours and don't be so bloody impertinent." Without saying another word and without hesitation Nicky turned over and raised herself onto her hands and knees. She nervously stuttered, "I'm ready when you want me Stuart." For about five minutes Stuart lay on his side looking at her, every so often he reached out and slapped her tits, at the same time he would say, "Let's get those nipples nice and hard that's a good girl." When the five minutes had passed he knelt up behind her and placed each of his hands on the inside of her thighs to force her legs apart saying, "Your fucking tight enough you cunt without kneeling with your legs together, do you understand?" "Yes Stuart, I'll make sure I don't do that again." Stuart slapped her across her buttocks really hard, she winced as he said, "Don't stop sucking me unless I say you can." "No Stuart I promise." She'd hardly finished saying it when he entered her hard enough to hear his thighs slap against her bottom. She let out a groan, but it was a groan of sheer pleasure. Stuart repeatedly withdrew and entered her time after time, as he did Nicky kept calling out, "Stuart I love you, don't stop fucking me, I love you, fuck me as long as you like, I love you Stuart, I love you."

Stuart lost count of how many times he withdrew and entered Nicky from behind but when he reached his climax it felt as though his cock was exploding with pleasure. He crumpled over onto his back. Nicky didn't move, she just knelt there motionless. Stuart spoke to her, "Nicky I've come, it's your turn now but you will have to kneel up straight in front of my face and use your hand to wank yourself off, I'm going to watch, can you do that?" "Yes

Stuart" she said and placed one knee either side of his chest with her clitoris almost touching his face. She began rubbing herself off just as he had told her. It wasn't very long before Stuart noticed that she was increasing the speed of rubbing herself and at the same time her body was starting to go rigid. Just at that moment Stuart reached around the back of her with his right hand and pressed his middle finger hard into the crack of her bottom. Nicky instantly let out a loud squeal of delight and at the same time the whole of her body quivered uncontrollably for what seemed to be a lifetime. She suddenly flopped forward and let her face come to rest on Stuart's shoulder. She whispered into his ear, "I've come darling and I love you, I love you, I love you." Almost at the same time Stuart enveloped her in his arms and said, "Ok babe, game over and I love you completely." After they had slept for a short while, still lying on the bed Nicky looked up into Stuart's eyes and said, "Thank you my darling I really enjoyed that and I hope you did as well?" "If you did my darling, then I did," he replied. Nicky looked longingly into his eyes again and said, "The final thing I want to say about this session my love is that I totally enjoyed it. I want you to know that I will do anything for you absolutely anything, I love you so much, I just don't want you to get fed up with me, tire of me or get bored with me, I love you and I will do anything for you." Stuart leaned over the top of her, gave her a passionate kiss and said, "It's time I made my way back."

Chapter 24
The Decision

Stuart returned to his room, he was pretty much shattered. He flopped backwards onto his bed and let his head come to rest on the pillow. He lay there with his hands clasped behind his head as usual. The only thing that he could think about whilst lying there was what an unbelievable session he had just spent with Nicky. He couldn't help thinking, "They don't come much better than that babe." With that thought on his mind he drifted into a relaxing sleep.

He woke up completely refreshed. He sat up and spun his legs around so that he was in a sitting position on the edge of his bed. He was just about to spring to his feet and make himself a coffee when he noticed that there was a message in green lights flashing on the wall next to the door. The message informed him that he could receive information from the Office for Unanswered Questions. Stuart realized immediately that they had soon arrived at a decision regarding his request for something to break the monotony that he occasionally had a problem with. He wasted no time in having a shower, some breakfast and setting off to the office. When he arrived there, he was expected and allowed in straight away. It seemed like minutes until he was now sitting facing Conrad again. Conrad looked at Stuart and began to speak, "Right then Stuart, your request has been considered by the committee and they have decided to offer you a mission in the correction squad." Stuart was suddenly unable to understand what Conrad was referring to. Without waiting for any time to pass he said, "Excuse me for interrupting you Conrad but may I ask what the correction squad is?" "Of course, Stuart," Conrad continued." You must remember that just before you were allowed into phase two you had to choose the destiny of someone you knew in phase one. Well occasionally the destiny chosen for someone is not carried out correctly, usually because the person chosen meets someone that they weren't meant to form a relationship with and it totally alters the chosen destiny that has been set out for them." On these occasions, we try to send someone from the correction squad back to phase one to try and break up the unplanned relationship. Actually Stuart, I am aware that you know someone in phase two extremely well who did suffer this fate." Stuart was again surprised, "Who's that?" he asked. Conrad smiled, "I believe you are acquainted with a young lady by the name of Nicky Clark." Stuart tried to disguise the total shock that he was feeling at that moment in time. He was extremely shocked because he was aware that the amazing session that he had just spent with Nicky was still very fresh in his mind. "Oh yes" he said, "I do know Nicky very well and I find her a very pleasant person to spend time with."

Conrad smiled again, "Yes Stuart of course you do, but now the reason we are talking about Nicky is because as you know Nicky was allowed into phase two on very special grounds. Basically, she was able to take up a different relationship than was meant to be in her chosen destiny." Conrad paused, before speaking again, "So Stuart, it has come to our attention that there is a young lady in phase one, her name is Keira Bradley, who is following in very similar footsteps to Nicky Clark. She has veered off her chosen destiny and is associating with a man named Frankie Dawson who is making Keira work as a prostitute. We have decided to send someone from phase two, back to phase one, to act on behalf of the correction squad in an attempt at getting Keira Bradley away from Frankie Dawson. Therefore, Stuart, the committee have decided that if you are still suffering from the boredom you mentioned during your last visit here they will allow you to take on this mission." Stuart sat there quite stunned at what he was hearing and was unable to make an immediate reply. After a couple of minutes of complete silence had passed Conrad continued speaking to Stuart.

"Now Stuart, before you make your final decision about whether you should accept this mission there are some very real dangers that you should know about. Therefore, if you choose to turn the mission down it will be totally understood and forgotten. I will now tell you what the dangers are. First, if there is any confrontation between you and anyone in phase one you should know that the person from phase one will always have the advantage over you because it is you that is not in the correct environment. The second danger that you need to know is that if you were to meet with a fatal accident whilst you are back in phase one, it is not possible to enter phase two for a second time. If you are successful in your mission you will drift off to sleep that night and when you wake up you will be back in your room in phase two." Conrad paused again, "That's it Stuart, you have fifteen minutes to make your decision." Within two minutes Stuart lifted his hands from off his lap folded his arms across his chest and immediately said, "I will definitely accept the mission, I am quite happy to help Keira in her unfortunate situation." Conrad opened the drawer in his desk, took out a file and passed it to Stuart. As Stuart took the file Conrad said, "Everything you need to know about Keira is in that file. Once you have read the file you will fall asleep, when you wake up you will be in phase one and in Keira's locality. The rest is up to you." Conrad didn't wait for a reply, he walked towards the door to leave saying, "You can go now Stuart, goodbye."

Chapter 25
Stuart's Mission

Stuart returned to his room, the first thing he did was to make himself a coffee. He put his coffee onto the small bedside table, lay back on his pillow and began studying the file that Conrad had given to him. It didn't take Stuart long to take in a lot of information about Keira and of course the file told him that the location where Keira was situated would be nowhere near his hometown. That was definitely a fact because Keira lived in Boston U.S.A. after moving there from New York about five years ago. As far as close relatives went all she had was a sister named Cory who still lived in New York. Unfortunately, there was one other person who now played a huge part in her life. That was the guy she lived with and who was the person responsible for making her prostitute herself whilst he pocketed the money, his name was Frankie Dawson.

After reading through the whole file Stuart was ready to drift off to sleep knowing full well that when he woke up he would be in his room but back in phase one. He decided there and then that when he woke up in phase one he would waste no time in the rescue of Keira. He had her photograph, he knew where she lived and he knew where she worked. His mission was now at the end of his sleep.

Upon waking up Stuart jumped out of bed and looked out of the window. He knew immediately, having been there before, that he was in the centre of Boston, he also knew immediately why he was there. He showered got dressed and drank his first coffee and wasted no time before shutting the front door behind him and setting off for Boston Way and the only diner in Boston called "The Eatery". That's where Keira worked behind the counter during the day. Stuart walked into the diner, straight up to the serving bar and sat on a high stool at the end of the bar next to the cash till. He guessed that would be the best place to sit so that he was able to start a conversation with Keira on a regular occasion. Keira walked up to him and said, "Morning cowboy what can I get ye?" She'd got long black hair about shoulder length. She was wearing a white blouse, a black mini skirt and black high heeled shoes. Her blouse was so open that he could see that she had large, but nice shaped breasts, and that she was wearing no bra. In fact, looking at the way she was dressed Stuart thought that she looked quite cheap. For some strange, unusual reason it caused him to feel the flicker of an erection.

Stuart quickly answered her question, "Yes honey, I will have a regular coffee and a large stack of pancakes with plenty of Maple Syrup." Stuart ate his pancakes drank his coffee and left. He returned the following day and ordered the same breakfast, in fact he repeated it for the next three days and on each day he would chat to her over the serving bar, trying to get to know her and hoping that she would quickly find him a friendly and trustworthy guy. On the fourth day he had just finished eating his pancakes and drinking his coffee, when he suddenly reached over the bar, grabbed hold of Keira's arm and said, "Keira honey, I know you won't understand but I've got something really important to tell you, so when you've finished today, if I could pick you up in my Dodge we could go and have a beer and I will explain." Keira leaned over the bar, flashing her tits again, she gave him a big smile, looked him straight in the eye and said, "Sure babe I finish at five o'clock."

Stuart pulled up outside the diner in his Dodge exactly on five o'clock, Keira was ready and waiting. Stuart flung the passenger door open and Keira jumped in. They didn't say an awful lot to each other before they arrived at the East Coast Hotel where they jumped out of the Dodge and went into the Hotel Bar where Stuart ordered a couple of beers. Keira picked her bottle of beer up, held it high and said, "Thanks Stuart I really do appreciate it." Stuart picked his beer up, held it high and returned the compliment. They both took a good swig of their beer and put the bottles on the table. Stuart wasted no time before saying, "Keira honey, I've got to tell you why I'm here as quickly as possible, ok." Keira nodded and Stuart continued, "The most important thing that I have to say is that I know everything that there is to know about you. For instance, the day you were born, where you were born, which of course is New York, and that both of your parents were killed in an automobile accident. The only living relative you have is a sister named Cory who still lives in New York and of course she is the reason that I know everything about you. Cory and myself have been really good friends for about the last four months. The reason she hasn't been in touch with you is because she's too embarrassed." Keira looked at him and said, "What do you mean Stuart, too embarrassed?" Stuart took Keira's hand in his and replied, "Because honey she knows that at night your boyfriend, Frankie Dawson, makes you work as a prostitute." He paused for a while, Keira blushed, then he continued, "The reason I'm here honey is because your sister Cory has pleaded with me to get you away from Frankie and away from Boston." Keira sniveled as she replied, "But Stuart I am so afraid of Frankie, he wouldn't hesitate to really hurt me if I stepped out of line." She started crying louder, Stuart put his arm around her and gave her a comforting hug, as he did he answered her, "I know he would honey that's why you have to let me help you get away tonight."

Keira looked directly into Stuart's eyes and said, "Ok Stuart what do I have to do?" Stuart went on to explain that she had to go home, pack immediately and meet him outside Dodo's shoe shop which was just down the street from the diner. He would be waiting for her with an overnight, one-way ticket on the railway that would take her to San Francisco. He would also give her the address of someone there who would set her up with a place to live, a job and keep a good look out for her. Keira gave Stuart a firm hug and as she turned to leave the bar she looked over her shoulder and shouted, "See you as soon as I can honey outside Dodo's."

Stuart jumped back into his Dodge and proceeded to drive back to Dodo's where he pulled up outside and waited. Just before 7.30pm he could see Keira walking towards Dodo's. She was wearing a very, very tight nylon sweater and a very short white ra-ra skirt with a red frill around the hem. She had obviously packed the few belongings that she was taking with her into the back pack that was wrapped around her shoulders. Stuart jumped out of the Dodge just as she approached. He walked up to her, put his arm around her waist, and said, "Well done babe you got back here pretty quick." A big smile spread across Keira's face as she replied, "Well it's a big adventure for me Stuart and to know that your helping me is even more special." Stuart suddenly took his arm from around her waist, gripped her arm just above the elbow, pulled her along the alley at the side of Dodo's and explained what was going to happen next. "Right babe, just behind Dodo's there is a railway track. We've got to walk along the track for a few minutes and we will come to the small railway station they've got here. We can jump up onto the platform and in about one hour's time the train that will take you all the way to San Francisco will stop here. You can get on that train and you will be away to safety. It will be mission accomplished, your sister will be happy, I will be happy and of course I'm hoping that you will be happy." They began their walk and just as they were passing a small siding that had two old unused carriages left there, Keira suddenly started pulling

Stuart towards her, sliding in between the two carriages. She spun around instantly to face Stuart and at the same time she said, "Stuart you are so good to help me like this, I have to repay you honey. Stuart, you can fuck me, fuck me really good." Before Stuart had a chance to say a word, Keira had wrapped her arms around his neck, jumped up and locked her ankles behind him so that she was locked around his waist, at the same time she whispered into his ear, I've left my panties off so that you can just get your cock out and fuck me." From that moment Stuart couldn't think about anything else. As soon as Keira had said "Fuck me," he had already formed an erection. His left arm went around her and beneath her skirt. With his left hand gripping her arse he reached down with his right hand, unzipped, took his manhood out of his pants and without any difficulty entered the wetness between her legs. Keira let out a little bit of a grunt whilst Stuart, pressing her and her backpack against the carriage, continued to fuck her with a frenzied animal lust. In less than three minutes Stuart had let out his groan of climax. Keira just hung around his neck and let him do his thing, as soon as she heard him groan she said, "Ok honey, if you're done you can put me down." Stuart didn't make any comment, he loosened the grip on her arse and let her slide her legs to the ground. He then reached down and put his spent cock back into his pants. Keira took a paper tissue from the arm of her sweater, wiped herself between the legs and threw it to the ground.

Chapter 26
Keira's Last Chance

Suddenly Keira screamed out, "Oh no, Frankie!" Stuart stood up straight quickly and spun around. Sure enough Frankie was standing there, he was wearing the usual leather jacket with zips all over it, he would never be seen without that jacket. Frankie replied to Keira, "Oh yes it's Frankie but," pointing at Stuart, "Who's this pussy pinching shit with you?" Before anyone had time to say anything Frankie raised his arm and threw a large rock that was probably bigger than a cricket ball. The rock was aimed at Stuart and it was right on target, it struck him just underneath his left eye. The blow from the rock struck him like a lightning bolt, Stuart fell backwards and rolled about nine metres down the railway embankment, coming to rest in the long grass at the bottom. Frankie rushed over and grabbed Keira by her hair at the back of her neck. He pulled her head backwards and snarled into her face, "Didn't I warn you once before that if you tried another trick like this I would split your face open?" Keira didn't say anything, all she could do was stand there in his grip. He snarled into her face again, "Don't you fucking remember me saying that to you, stupid bitch?" Keira nodded and sounding terrified muttered, "Yes Frankie." Frankie immediately spun around and as hard as he could, slammed Keira's face into the side of the carriage. All down the side of her nose and lip burst wide open and blood spurted up and over the filthy carriage windows. He threw her to the ground shouting, "Get yourself over to that fucking van as quick as you can." He then bent down and picked up a dirty, rust covered crow bar that would have been used to remove old railway sleepers. It was about two and a half metres long, he turned and headed down the embankment towards Stuart, gripping it in his right hand. When he reached the bottom of the slope he stood over the top of Stuart and glared down at him. Stuart was looking up but with one hand over the wound underneath his right eye, he was still wincing from the pain. Frankie spit on his face and then spoke, "You interfering shit, you need someone to teach you to know what's good for you and that you would have been much better off to stay where you were." Frankie spat into Stuart's face again. Gripping the crow bar in both of his hands he raised it above his head. He held it there for a few seconds before bringing the pointed end down with such force and aimed it directly at Stuart's abdomen that it completely penetrated Stuart's body and pinned him to the ground. Stuart didn't make a sound other than a stifled gurgle as blood trickled down his chin. Frankie turned and climbed up the embankment. Stuart could just about hear him as he reached Keira, who was still kneeling with blood oozing from her face, he shouted at her, "Right slut, you get over to that van quick, you've got double working hours tonight and it's going to be on your belly." Stuart passed out, he reopened his eyes just as the sun was rising over the top of the embankment. Obviously, he wasn't feeling too good but he could still comprehend his situation. He put his hand around the crow bar at the point where it had entered his abdomen, he raised his hand up and looked at it. His hand was totally covered in blood, black blood. He could remember Keira and he could remember his mission and he obviously understood that his mission had failed. It was then that he realized that after being wounded he had passed out and he knew that he had just woken up. He was feeling tired again and was preparing to nod off for a rest, only this time he was hoping to wake up back in his room in phase two. Just then he coughed from his belly, some blood spurted up into the air from out of his mouth and splashed over his face. He could feel himself gently falling to sleep with the pleasant thought on his mind. I hope I wake up so that I can go for a stroll in the Hall of Second Greetings.

The End.

Printed in Great Britain
by Amazon